THE MUSE

L.M. HALLORAN

Contents

Copyright

Copyright © 2017 by L.M. Halloran.

Cover Photography from **Shutterstock.com**

ISBN : 979-8-9864180-6-3

lmhalloran.com

for the survivors

Part I

1. aesthetics

The three flights of stairs before me might as well be Everest, only instead of snow and rocks barring my way, it's students loitering before their first class of the quarter.

Like them, I'm late. Unlike them, I hate being late. Especially today, as my class is a thousand times more important than whatever introductory English course these fresh-faced undergrads are too lazy to reach on time.

For starters, I'm not a student. At least not at the moment. I'm supposed to be assistant teaching a small group of English majors in a classroom that still, after two flights of stairs, seems to be a continent away.

On the plateau before my final ascension, I'm confronted by a group hogging the space. They're talking and laughing loudly, unmindful of those of us who actually give a shit about academics.

"Excuse me, please!"

Despite my lofty graduate-student status, no one bothers moving. I'm forced to dive through them like I'm spelunking instead of mountain climbing. Not an uncommon occurrence, unfortunately. I blame my mother, who bestowed upon me her diminutive stature, pale blonde hair, and perpetually fey features.

A glance at my watch tells me I have less than a minute until I'm going to make a terrible first impression on the professor.

I break into a run, messenger bag bouncing against my hip as I dart up the final staircase and down a rapidly emptying hallway. Ignoring the twinge in my bad knee, I skid to a stop before the desired door and yank it open.

Thank God.

Pre-class antics are still taking place. Students are chatting, slapping notebooks and pencils on desks, fiddling with smartphones, or surreptitiously slurping coffee and munching breakfast bars.

A glance toward the head of the room gives me my first look at Professor James S. Beckett, who was supposed to be at the faculty luncheon yesterday but never showed. On paper he's scary as hell: acclaimed poet, award-winning, New York Times Bestselling author of crime fiction, and newly appointed Director of the Creative Writing Program.

Thanks to borderline-obsessive Google searching, I know what he looks like. But all I can see right now is longish brown hair tousled to the kind of accidental perfection normally not seen out of magazine spreads. His face is downturned, eyes on the open notebook on his desk. He writes furiously, the movements harsh and slashing. *Left-handed.*

As I walk closer, I have an unhealthy urge to snatch the notebook away and read it.

"Professor Beckett?" I ask breathlessly.

He grunts, not looking up. A glance back at the class shows me faces angled toward us in curiosity. Some are familiar from previous courses, and I trade a few smiles.

"Are you going to talk or just stand there?"

The rude question is made irritatingly musical by a smooth British accent. My head whips back around, a flush rising to my face.

"I'm sorry?" I squeak, then clear my throat. "I'm Iris Eliot. Your TA."

The pen finally stops moving—it's not a slow fading of mind-body transfer but a savage stop. His head comes up, vivid green eyes narrowing on my face. I stop breathing for a few moments, feeling like an insect under a pin. The dissection of my person lasts long enough that I hear students begin to whisper.

Then, with no shift in expression, he glances over my shoulder toward the wall clock. "You're late," he says sharply, and stands with a screech of wooden chair legs to address the class.

Still frozen like a brainless golem beside his desk, I watch him similarly dissect the fifteen faces seated before him.

"If you're here, it means you want to be writers. Maybe you want to teach, too, but this class isn't about teaching. It's about writing."

Stalking around the desk, he leans against it to cross arms over his sweater-clad chest. After another sweep of his gaze across the classroom, he continues, "If even the smallest part of you is unsure about your identity as a writer, pack up your things now." He points at a student in the front row, a mousy girl not more than twenty-one, with thick glasses and lustrous dark hair. "Are you a writer?"

She turns beet red, mouth opening soundlessly. Finally, she gasps, "Yes."

Beckett nods, gaze swerving to the back of the room. "How about you? Yes, you, the young man with gum in his mouth, a bad shave, and greasy hair."

I wince, my eyes finding the shocked student's face.

A wad of white gum is stuck to his bottom molars, visible inside his open mouth.

"Uhh—" he starts.

"Nope," snaps Beckett. "Get out."

The student flushes. "I'm an English major—"

"Creative Writing focus?" grates Beckett.

"Uhh, no—"

"Out!"

The command snaps like a whip, and a second later the student gathers his belongings and rushes out the door. I stare after him, then turn to glare at Professor Beckett. If there's one type of person I truly loathe, it's a bully.

I'm so incensed, I don't care that he's already looking at me, brows raised in inquiry. When I recognize the glint in his eyes as amusement, I lose my shit.

"You can't do that!"

His lips curl, but I hesitate to call it a smile. A snarl, more like. "Oh, can't I? Are you a writer, Iris Eliot?"

"Yes," I snap.

Satisfaction flares in his eyes. "There," he says, jerking a thumb in my direction as he addresses the class. "*That* is the response of a writer. How about you—third row. Yes, you. Are you a writer?"

"Yes? I mean, yes!" The soft voice grows firmer.

"You?"

"Y-yes."

"Weak, but there's fire in your eyes so I'll let you stay...."

He continues until every student has answered in the affirmative, their voices gaining in confidence until the last virtually shouts the response. Beckett grins his approval, the expression so transforming that my lips part in soundless awe.

Surly and scowling, he could pass as a prematurely crotchety forty. Grinning, however, he looks his age. Thirty-three, if my memory serves. And every bit as handsome as Google warned.

"Ms. Eliot, are you going to stand there for the next fifty minutes or would you like to take a seat?"

I blink away cobwebs of scandalous thoughts and realize he's caught me staring. That snarly half-smile is back. My cheeks burning, I grip my bag tight to my side and stride to the back of the classroom to claim a desk. As Beckett begins his first-class spiel, I set up my laptop, listening with half an ear until I hear my name.

"...will send you an email with her office hours. The workshops for this class are Tuesday and Thursday mornings. Ms. Eliot will be sending me weekly assessments of your participation and progress, so do take her seriously. Unless you're suffering from a debilitating disease, I recommend you attend every one. If you don't, you'll see your lack of commitment reflected in your final grade. I also plan on spot checking the workshops myself." Another lightning-flash of a grin. "Not even Ms. Eliot will know which ones I plan to attend."

As he continues rattling on about syllabus, midterm and final projects, and weekly journaling assignments, I eventually grow used to his accented, rapid-fire speech. I even muse that his voice matches how he writes. Concise. Eloquent. Cutting.

Thinking of his smile, I add another adjective.

Dangerous.

"—all I have. Any questions?"

No one moves.

Beckett nods shortly. "Very well. Journals out. Twenty minutes of freestyle writing to be turned in at the end of class. Stop staring at me and start now. First impressions matter." His eyes, electric emerald in the sunlight dancing through the nearest window, find my face. "Ms. Eliot, if you'll join me in the hallway a moment?"

Taking a steadying breath, I close my laptop and stand. *You can't quit. You need the TA stipend. You need to finish your Masters. One more year. You can do this. However brilliantly talented and obnoxiously handsome he might be, he's just a man. More importantly, he's the freaking head of your program. Be professional.*

Bolstered by my internal pep talk, I follow Beckett's tall frame into the empty hallway. The door snicks closed behind us, sounding disproportionally ominous. Arms once again crossed over his chest, he stares down at me, a frown puckering the skin between his eyebrows.

"Aren't you a little young for a graduate student in her final year?"

The question triggers a lifetime's worth of emotional baggage and professionalism flies out the window. "Are you joking? Is there an age requirement I'm unaware of?"

His lips do an odd, quirking dance; I think he might be trying not to smile. "How old *are* you?"

I gape. "Didn't you read the Code of Conduct? You're not supposed to discriminate based on age, sex, orientation—"

He waves a hand imperiously. "Fine, don't tell me. And call me Beck or Beckett. Professor makes me think of graybeards with food in their teeth. Did you get all my emails?"

The abrupt shift in topics sends my already malfunctioning head-to-mouth filter into full meltdown. "Sure did. All eight hundred of them."

Oh my God, I'm so fired.

But to my shock, his eyes crinkle with mirth. "You're

a cheeky one, aren't you? I was told you'd have no other assignments beyond your course load. Is that correct?"

I nod again, less enthusiastically. What mere weeks ago had seemed like a gift from the heavens has degraded in the last fifteen minutes to a silent plea of, *Please let me survive this quarter.*

By the amount of work he's assigned the students and his insistence that his TA have no other duties, I'm now relatively certain he wants me to be his assistant-bitch for the next twelve weeks.

And we're off to such a promising start.

When he doesn't say anything else, merely pinning me with his focused stare, I feel my neck heating beneath my scarf. Whatever his thoughts, the look he's giving me is *not* appropriate between teacher and student.

At length, he murmurs, "You seem familiar."

"Familiar how?" I ask nervously.

He blinks, shaking his head a little. "We haven't met before? You *are* over eighteen, aren't you?"

In a flash of sickening insight, I recall a particularly lurid article about his reputation as a whiskey-swilling philanderer.

He thinks I'm a one-night stand.

Ew.

"We haven't met," I say forcefully, then summon a

modicum of the poise I've been lacking since I slept through my six a.m. alarm. "Professor, I'm very much looking forward to assisting you this quarter. Did you receive my schedule and contact information?"

He nods. "It's Beckett or Beck. And I did, thank you. I saw that you're also taking my Advanced Fiction Writing class Wednesday evenings. And you're on my docket for a meeting tomorrow, is that correct?"

"Yes, to review progress on my thesis."

Which will probably end in me stabbing myself in the eye with a pencil.

"Good, good. Seems we'll be seeing a lot of each other for the foreseeable future." He reaches for the door handle, flashing that dangerous grin at me. "The former Director spoke very highly of you, Ms. Eliot. I look forward to learning what makes you tick."

On that titillating and terrifying note, he sweeps back into the room. I stare at the floor, realizing several disturbing truths at once.

1. My heart is racing a mile a minute.

2. My knees are weak.

3. I haven't felt this alive in years.

<u>2. allegory</u>

The sights, sounds, and smells of White Harp Pub on University Ave are a balm for my tired brain and eyes. Holed up in a booth with my roommate Claire and her boyfriend, Monty, I feel the day's stress draining away at the same rate as my pint. Every crack of a pool cue on a ball, laughter from neighboring tables, or cheer from around the dartboards further elevates my mood toward contentment.

"So yeah," I conclude my rehashing of this morning's debacle, "I was late, didn't have coffee or breakfast, and looked and acted like a hot mess. Awesome first impression."

Claire's hazel eyes dance with mischief. "Were you really wearing your brother's sweatshirt?"

I roll my eyes. "Yes. I couldn't find my coat. And yes,

I know I look like a kid in daddy's shirt when I wear it." Which is more apt than either of them know, as my brother had a more substantial role in my upbringing than my father.

Derrick's faded high school hockey sweatshirt is my personal talisman. When I need strength or courage, or an imagined hug from my big brother, all I have to do is put it on.

As the sweatshirt has never failed me, this morning was obviously a fluke.

To redirect my thoughts, I ask Claire, "How was teaching?"

A fellow graduate student, she's pursuing a Masters in Philosophy, and like me has taken on the punishing (and rewarding) life of a teaching assistant. Unlike me, however, she's teaching her own class, an introductory Philosophy course.

"Besides spilling coffee down my blouse right before the lecture?" she asks defeatedly.

I grimace in sympathy. "I saw the shirt soaking in the sink. That sucks, Claire."

Monty, also a Philosophy grad student, looks up from the textbook on the table before him. "It wasn't that bad. You couldn't even see it under the scarf."

Claire groans and drains her beer, then gives me a

meaningful look. "It was his scarf. The cable-knit lime green one."

I bite my lips in effort to thwart a grin. "Don't worry, your students won't remember it a week from now." From Claire's answering glare, she knows as well as I do that I'm lying.

First impressions are handprints in cement. Only jackhammers can erase them. There's a high chance that most of her students will forever think of her as Lime Green.

"I heard someone call me Limey as they were leaving," she says miserably.

I bite my lips harder, but it's no use. My burst of laughter makes Claire scowl at first, but eventually she giggles, and then like delinquents in a church pew we suddenly can't stop laughing. As usual, Monty is late to the festivities and watches us in befuddlement.

A solid two minutes later, I'm wiping the tears of mirth from my eyes when I hear Monty say in an awed tone, "Professor Beckett, how are you this evening? Monty Nelson. We met outside the faculty lounge this morning?"

My fingers, which froze at the sound of his name, lower from my eyes in time for me to see the men shake hands.

Beckett nods, smiling slightly. "Ah, yes, I remember. You were wearing a rather memorable scarf."

I make the mistake of looking at Claire, and we burst into helpless laughter again. Pressing my palms to my mouth to shut myself up, I lift my gaze to the famous writer currently staring at me with a vaguely unsettled expression.

In dark jeans and a worn leather jacket, with a grey scarf wound around his neck, he looks like something I want to climb and swing on.

He's the Director of the Creative Writing Program.

Head of the Thesis Committee.

My BOSS.

I give my left cheek a light, reviving slap. Before I can give the same treatment to my other cheek, Claire grabs my raised hand and yanks it under the table.

"Ms. Eliot," says Beckett, still frowning slightly, "are you quite all right? Shouldn't you be preparing for the first workshop tomorrow morning?"

I straighten in my seat. "I'm fully prepared, Professor Beckett."

His eyes flicker downward before snapping back to my face. He frowns harder, and beneath the table, Claire's fingers squeeze the blood from mine.

Into the awkward silence, Monty asks, "Would you care to join us, professor?"

Beckett's gaze stays fixed on me. "Maybe next time," he says curtly, and spins on his heel to stalk toward the exit.

Claire releases a noisy breath. "Holy *shit* he's hot."

"Hey!" admonishes Monty.

Claire gives him a quick kiss on the cheek, then faces me, eyes widened hugely. "Did you see what I saw? He totally checked out the girls."

I glance down at my cleavage, relieved to see minimal exposure. "No, he didn't. He must have been looking at my necklace."

Claire snorts. The words sound thin to me as well, and after a moment, I accept that my *foreseeable future* just became monumentally more challenging.

Groaning, I push my empty pint glass away and gather my notebook and purse.

Claire wears a knowing smirk. "You're going home to review for tomorrow, aren't you?"

I nod, sliding out of the booth and standing to put on my coat. "After this winning second impression, he now thinks I'm a drunken idiot who tripped and fell into the MFA program."

Claire giggles, scooting closer to Monty and dropping her chin onto his shoulder. He absentmindedly pats her dark hair, gaze unwavering from his textbook.

"Walk safe. See you in a bit."

"Will do."

With a final wave, I weave through the scattered crowd—a mostly mellow mix of graduate students, laypersons, and the occasional faculty member. Being far removed from Greek Row and the more modern, raucous bars closer to the university, the White Harp has been a favorite of Claire's and mine since our undergrad years.

As I step into the brisk night air, I say a silent prayer that James Beckett never returns.

"Ms. Eliot."

I shriek at his voice behind me. As I spin around, the heel of my boot slips on damp concrete. *No, please no...* My arms cartwheel for balance, my purse flying from my wrist. As my fight for balance is officially lost, I close my eyes tightly in preparation for a bruised ass and ego.

Hands seize my coat in opposition of gravity. For a second I'm airborne, then I crash into a wall. A leather-clad, human wall.

"Good Lord, woman," he bites out, "you're a disaster."

I open one eye at a time, just in case the universe decides to save me from myself in the interim. It doesn't, and I stare up at Beckett's face from an alarming three-inch distance. Under the pub's exterior lights, I can see the stubble on his jaw. I'm just buzzed—or stupid—

enough to imagine what it would feel like on my cheek. And other places.

His fingers clenching on my arms bring me back from the edge of insanity. I stiffen, and he abruptly loosens his hold. Dragging a hand through his hair, he mutters something under his breath.

"What?" I ask.

He glares at me. "I said, *I asked for a man.*"

It takes me a few seconds, but then I understand. Hot anger burns through the vestiges of my embarrassment. "I don't know what your TAs at Boston University were like, but here in Washington we don't lift our skirts for our professors. Consider yourself safe from my lascivious intents."

His mouth opens, closes, and finally quirks. "I should think you don't wear skirts very often, given the weather." He glances at the misty sky. "In fact, it's not too dissimilar from England."

I stare at him mutely, shaking my head, then turn to gather the contents of my purse from the sidewalk. He crouches beside me, offering me several pens. We work in silence for a few moments—in which I'm grateful no tampons spilled—before he clears his throat.

"Lascivious intents? A bit of a mouthful, that."

I risk a glance at his face, and the sight of his merry

eyes makes me crack a smile. "That was pretty bad, I'll admit."

He grins, a flash of white teeth in the shadows. "You might have said instead, *Sod off, you misogynistic prick.*"

Improbably, I laugh. And when he offers his hand to help me to my feet, I take it. He releases me quickly, but the echo of his warm skin stays on my palm.

"Thanks for, uh, catching me."

"Since the impending accident was my fault, it was the least I could do." His smile slowly fades, eyebrows pinching. "I apologize for my comment, Ms. Eliot. I did ask for a man, but not for the reason you assumed. I merely wanted to avoid the rumor mill. Given your reference to Boston University, I'm assuming you know why I left?"

My stomach drops as I realize there's no way around the truth. "You had an affair with a student."

He nods. "I did," he says without shame. "I was twenty-eight, high off my rising success, and criminally self-centered. I very nearly ruined a young woman's academic career."

I frown. "Why are you telling me this?"

He doesn't move, but I suddenly feel like he's looming over me. I shiver in my coat and clutch my purse tighter to my chest.

"You know exactly why. Because this," a finger jerks between our chests, "is what they call chemistry. So I'm going to say this once and one time only: do *not* tempt me."

Heat frissons through me even as I stiffen in affront. "Are you kidding? Tempt you? I should report you!"

He chuckles. "To whom? Your Director?"

"The Head of the Graduate Department," I snap.

Beckett shakes his head chidingly. "Joseph and I were undergrads together at Stanford."

"My God," I breathe, "you're an absolute—"

"Prick," he finishes with another sharp smile. "Yes, I know. It's a defect I have yet to remedy."

The door of the pub opens and closes.

"Iris, is that you?" asks Claire. "I thought you were going home."

Beckett gives me a final, searing glance before striding down the sidewalk. Claire moves up beside me, and we stare at his diminishing figure.

"Was that—"

"Yep," I say.

"Why do you look so flustered?"

Because this is what they call chemistry.

"I'm fine," I lie. "He just lectured me again about his expectations for the quarter."

"Lame. Do you think he's going to monitor you tomorrow?"

I finally look at her. "I really hope not."

"**W**ell, is anyone going to comment on Terrance's piece?"

I look over the classroom, noting the students who meet my eyes and those who stare at their desks. When no one says anything, I wring my mental hands. Despite Beckett's warning, I can already tell they're not taking me seriously.

Chin up, buttercup, whispers my brother's voice. *You'll always be underestimated, so you might as well come out of the gate swinging.*

I sigh loudly, complete with groan. "Okay, people. In case your brains malfunctioned, we just listened to an extended metaphor about an infected nose ring. Did you like it? Did it make sense? Greg, talk!"

Greg jerks in his seat, then clears his throat. "Yes, it

made sense. It was gross, but that kind of made it more appealing."

My gaze scans the room. "Janice? You look like you're sucking on a lemon. Why didn't you like it?"

She shrugs. "It was well written, and I like that he used something not clichéd to represent a broken heart. But like Greg said, it was gross. Gross in a distracting way, like by the end I wasn't thinking about heartbreak but getting the poor guy a tissue and some peroxide."

The class laughs, even Terrance. "Tone down gross-factor, check."

The nicest feature of senior writing students is that by now, they're used to critiques. There's nothing quite as irritating as crying freshman. I should know—I used to be one.

I glance at the clock. "Okay. Fifteen minutes to work on Beckett's assignment due Monday. And don't forget to pair up with a proofreader. Even if you think you're Hemingway, you need a reader."

I veer around the desk and sit, pulling out my notebook and grabbing a pen. After a quick review of Thursday's lesson plan, I retrieve my thesis proposal and read it for the billionth time. My meeting with Beckett is right after class. At least his office is in the same building, so I can avoid a repeat of yesterday's sweaty-mess performance.

In fact, my attire today screams *demure professional*. White blouse, grey slacks, black cardigan, my long hair drawn back into a sleek ponytail. My only concession to personality are my bright red flats; after last night's slippage, heels and I are on a hiatus.

The closer the minute hand moves toward 10:50, the higher my anxiety ratchets. So does the noise from the hallway as other classes let out.

After several questioning glances, I relent. "See you Thursday." Everyone gathers their things, waving or saying goodbye as they hurry from the room.

When the last student is gone, I slide my notebook into my bag and prepare to face down Beckett.

The door opens suddenly, revealing the man in question. My heart leaps alarmingly. He's wearing faded jeans that cling to all the right places and a black dress shirt sans tie. Messy hair, scruffy face, ink-stained left hand.

God help me.

"Ms. Eliot, we're taking our meeting to the HUB. I'm starved."

"W-what?" I stammer.

He frowns. "I spoke English, didn't I? Hustle. I'm yours for thirty minutes."

Then he disappears into the hallway, final words thrumming in my head and body. *Damnit, why does he have to be so good looking?* The universe doesn't answer. Or the silence is answer enough.

Beckett is fiddling with his phone at the top of the stairs. His hair looks even more chaotic than it did a minute ago. Bracing myself for the impact of his eyes, I walk up to him.

"Professor, I really don't feel comfortable—"

"Oh, stop," he says lightly, not looking up. "Did you bring your manuscript? I've already reviewed your proposal and want you to read me an excerpt." He finally deigns to meet my gaze; after a moment, his brows lift. "Hello?"

Unstoppable heat floods my face. "I have it on my laptop, yes, but—"

"Then quit dallying."

He tucks his phone into his back pocket and heads down the stairs. Students file past. I don't *want* to notice, but of course I do—every female devours him head to toe. Just like I'm doing my damnedest not to.

Do not *tempt me.*

Clearly that should have been my line.

When I catch up to him at the bottom of the stairs, he barely pauses before we head outside into the cool air. The sky is a vapid blue, the sun hiding behind trees.

"You should be wearing a coat," he mumbles.

My gaze snaps to him. "I'm not cold."

"Yes, you are."

With dawning embarrassment, I look down, then yank my cardigan over my chest. He chuckles, dark and low, the sound lifting goosebumps and tightening my nipples even further.

"Congratulations, by the way, Ms. Eliot. You look at least twenty-four today."

I roll my eyes. "I'm twenty-seven."

He nods, flashing me a tight grin. "I read your file."

"Great," I droll.

Laughing, he opens the door to the student union and gestures me before him. Still gripping my sweater closed, I duck inside. As I pass him, my nose fills with his subtle cologne. I might be imagining things, but I think I hear his swift, indrawn breath.

Did we just smell each other?

Nerves exploding in my stomach, I step outside the flow of traffic and try to catch my breath. The mere thought of reading an excerpt of my novel to him makes my fingers and toes tingly.

"What do you feel like?" he asks, glancing around the various cafes. "Burger? Salad? Soup?"

"Soup's fine," I force out.

Somehow, I survive the ordering process with Beckett standing behind me, close enough that I feel his shirt whispering along my back. It's not his fault—it's packed in here. When someone bumps him, and he draws flush to my body, arousal plummets through me and every muscle in my body locks.

"Sorry," he murmurs, stepping quickly back.

By the time we have our food and find a table, I can't think straight much less look him in the face. Nor can I taste my soup, which by some miracle doesn't end up on my blouse. To make matters even worse, every few minutes a faculty member stops by the table—every one of them women wearing too much perfume and breathing too heavily.

When the most recent applicant for Beckett's bed leaves, I check my watch. "We'll have to reschedule. That last conversation was six minutes of mind numbing innuendo too many."

To my surprised glee, a flush blooms on his cheekbones. "I'm sorry, Ms. Eliot."

"Oh, please," I say with a dismissive wave. "You obviously love it. I've never seen so many faculty eating lunch at the HUB. Let me guess, you come here every day."

Still looking chagrined, he nods. "I like the atmosphere. The faculty lounges are stuffy and boring."

I bend for my bag. "Okay, well—"

"You don't have class until one," he says abruptly. "Let's get coffee."

I still, my eyes narrowing. "You said you had thirty minutes."

He shrugs. "I lied."

As I stare at him, he stands and moves around the table to— "Are you seriously trying to pull my chair back for me?" I ask, arching my neck to see his face.

His eyes fasten for an electric moment on my throat. "Merely doing the gentlemanly thing. Up you go."

Flustered, I jerk to standing and lurch away from the chair. My foot snags in the strap of my bag, but before I can fall on my face Beckett grabs my arm. His sudden grin knocks the air from my chest.

"Have you always been such a klutz?"

I pry my arm from his grip as subtly as I can. "Yes," I lie.

With a too-knowing smile lingering on his lips, he hands me my bag. I head for the onsite Starbucks, not looking to see if he follows.

Ten minutes later, we're back outside. Beckett takes the lead, guiding me around a few buildings and into a small garden. Several benches are occupied, but there's one set in a cave of greenery that's empty. Probably because it's freezing in the shade.

Beckett drops sinuously onto the bench, taking up altogether too much space. I stare warily at the remaining seat.

He sighs. "Come on, I don't bite. Let's just forget about my crass words last night. I had a pint too many. You're lovely—truly—but I'm not going to try to shag you. You're perfectly safe from me."

Not feeling safe *at all*, I sit beside him. The warmth from his body radiates onto my side, igniting a dangerous need to curl into him. Instead, I bend forward to set down my coffee and pull my laptop from my bag. My movements are graceless, and as I straighten the side of my breast brushes his knee. Said knee jerks away.

"Sorry," I gasp, and yank upright.

He clears his throat. "Alright, let's have it. Your proposal sounded interesting. Read me the first three paragraphs."

Opening my laptop, I enter my password and retrieve my manuscript from the desktop. Familiar words fill the screen, yet in this moment—with this man beside me—they are utterly foreign. Doubt crawls through me, making my fingers shake on the trackpad. Unmoving, I wait for courage, wishing I was wearing my brother's sweatshirt.

With an aggravated sigh, Beckett unceremoniously snatches my laptop and plops it on his knees. Leaning forward, his eyes rapidly scan the text. He quickly reads the first page, a finger confidently scrolling down. In less than two minutes, he's finished the first chapter.

He gently closes the laptop and stares across the garden.

My heart is pounding so hard I can hear it. "You hate it," I whisper, startled by the depth of my devastation.

After another few moments, he blinks and looks at me. I can't decipher his expression. "Not at all. It's not bad. A little verbose, perhaps. The bit at the end, about her brother's hand in hers, was quite arresting." He glances away, then back, eyes narrowing. Assessing and dissecting. "Is your brother still alive?"

Cold spirals in my chest and outward, turning my lips numb. *How did he...*

"Is the accident in my file?"

"I don't know anything about an accident," he replies gently, eyes steady on mine. "I merely wondered, given the autobiographical tone and foreshadowing."

Unable to maintain eye contact, I turn away. My movement has the unfortunate side effect of bringing my back against his arm. Ignoring the line of heat, I stare at the leaves on a nearby bush until the urge to cry passes.

"How long ago was this accident?" he asks softly.

Eleven years, six months, and four days.

"I'd rather not talk about it," I say, turning to meet his gaze. "Do you have any other suggestions besides monitoring verbosity?"

He stares hard at me for another moment, then

smiles. "There were a few instances of passive voice that could be active."

"It's used for effect."

His smile grows at my defensiveness. "Is it finished?"

"Yes."

"Word count?"

"Ninety-thousand."

"Good," he says, nodding shortly. "Email me the pdf. I'll read it tonight. Let's set up a meeting for early next week. At least three hours. I'll walk you through any notes I have."

"Okay," I say weakly, accepting my laptop from his hands.

He retrieves his coffee from the ground and uses his free hand to send his hair into another orbit. "Right, then. Have a good day, Ms. Eliot. And for the love of God, buy a bloody coat." He walks away without another glance.

I look down, see the clear outlines of my nipples through my blouse, and drop my head into my hands.

4. antithesis

*N*ot until I'm getting ready for bed do I remember Beckett's request for my manuscript. It's nearing eleven o'clock but figuring it's better sent late than never, I draw my laptop onto the bed and open my email. In addition to the expected spam, I see a message from an unfamiliar, non-university address.

Unfamiliar, yes, but not unrecognizable: j.s.beck. The subject line reads, *Don't be a coward,* and when I open it, there's no other content.

"I guess the message is clear enough," I mutter, and hurriedly attach my manuscript and send it.

Seconds later, a chat box pops up in the corner of the screen.

j.s.beck: *About damned time.*

iris_el: *You didn't specify when I had to send it, just that you wanted it tonight.*

j.s.beck: *Is your sass a defense mechanism for looking like an underaged forest nymph?*

My mouth drops open.

iris_el: *Are you drunk?*

j.s.beck: *Possibly. Did you buy a coat?*

My nipples tingle in response. "Don't do it, don't do it," I tell myself, even as my fingers fly over the keyboard and like an automaton, I hit Send.

Frozen, my heart pounding, I wait. The cursor blinks at me like an oracle of judgement, then a tiny chime sounds. My eyes snap to his reply.

j.s.beck: *I wouldn't have to think about your breasts if they were where they should be.*

I frown in confusion.
Another chime.

j.s.beck: *Several places come to mind. In my mouth. Smashed on my chest. Or bouncing in my face.*

"Holy shit," I whisper, as heat funnels straight to my core.

At a soft knock on my bedroom door, I slam my laptop shut. "Come in, Claire," I call hoarsely.

She pops her head inside the room. "I saw your light —Why is your face red?"

"I was, uh, rubbing it."

Her eyes narrow, flickering to the laptop beside me. "I thought I heard you talking. Were you Skyping your mom?"

"Nope, just muttering to myself."

She doesn't look convinced, but after a moment gives me a tired smile. "Okay, goodnight. See you in the morning."

"Yep, 'night."

The door closes and I open the laptop warily. There's a new message.

j.s.beck: *I've scared you off, haven't I?*

Somewhere in my rational mind, I know this is wrong. So risky. But the long-dormant, reckless half of me is wide awake and in control. I haven't felt this way in years. Wanton. Desirous. It's a gift I won't—can't— give back.

iris_el: *No. I was merely admiring the assets in question.*

j.s.beck: *Isn't that a pretty picture. Tell me, Ms. Eliot, are your nipples as I imagine them? Tight, rosy little buds?*

My hips twitch, driving my pulsing center against the bed. With a shaking hand, I pull up my t-shirt to expose my breasts. Feeling possessed, I pinch one of the aching peaks and swallow a moan.

iris_el: *Yes. Very sensitive to stimulus.*

j.s.beck: *I'll use more tongue than teeth, then.*

The mental picture of his dark head over my chest, sucking and licking, shoots shocks of pleasure through my groin.

iris_el: *Don't stop now.*

He doesn't disappoint, sentences filling the screen at a rapid pace.

j.s.beck: *I start on that white swan's neck, tonguing your pulse and that little hollow long enough that you lose patience. You grab for me, but I capture your wrists* *and drag them over your head. We're both nervous I'm too big for you, but nothing short of the apocalypse is going to keep us from finding out.*

Your whole body is flushed and trembling. As I work my way down your soft belly, you make small, strangled sounds. They give me a feeling of savage triumph, because I know how badly you want to scream and how much you don't want to give me that victory.

I finally release your hands to spread your thighs for my ravenous mouth. Your fingers sink into my hair and yank, forcing my tongue deep inside you. When you begin to beg, all my well-laid plans collapse. I can't wait any longer. Sitting back on my heels, I yank you into my arms, dragging my...

I stare at the blinking cursor, panting and poised on the edge of climax. I can't wait for him to start typing again—so I don't. Three more purposeful movements of my hand and an orgasm unfolds, so consuming I arch backward to smother my cry with a pillow.

Lazy heat swirling through my limbs, I roll onto my side to stare at the computer screen. Finally, another sentence comes, and it brings a gratified smile to my lips.

j.s.beck: *Seems I'm not as coordinated as I thought.*
iris_el: *You got the job done, professor.*
j.s.beck: *Gah, please don't call me that.*
iris_el: *Fine... Beckett.*
j.s.beck: *Better. In twelve weeks, you can call me James.*
iris_el: *Why?*
j.s.beck: *Because the second this quarter is over, I'm going to fuck you until neither of us can walk.*

My breath dies, my body throbs, and my rational brain wakes up. With shaking fingers, I type my response.

iris_el: *We'll see.*
j.s.beck: *Yes, we will. Until tomorrow evening, Ms. Eliot.*

Grey text informs me that j.s.beck is offline.

"Oh my God, what did I just do?" I whisper.

____

By the time I walk into class the following evening, I'm half-convinced last night was a dream. I'm sure that somewhere on my computer the chat between j.s.beck and myself is logged, but I'm also sure I don't have the guts to read it in the light of day.

Somehow, I have to get through Advanced Fiction Writing with Beckett. Not as my advising professor or thesis chair, but as my *teacher*. The class is only one day a week, which is a blessing, but because of its infrequency it's the ungodly length of two hours and fifty minutes.

With ten minutes to spare before the seven o'clock start, I enter the room and veer toward the back. Most of the students are familiar—there aren't that many of us in the MFA Creative Writing Program—and I drop into a seat beside Griffen Banks.

"Hey, Iris, how was your summer?"

"Peachy. Did you go back to Houston like you talked about?"

He nods, brown eyes warming. "Yeah, it was great. Can't wait to move back permanently. How about you? You're from San Francisco, right?"

"Yep, but Seattle's home now. Plus, I did a summer internship at Fox Publishing. Fingers crossed for a job offer at the end of the year."

His brows lift. "Awesome, I remember you mentioning that you were going to interview."

We don't notice that the room's gone quiet until

Beckett says, "If you're done flirting, Ms. Eliot and Mr. Banks?"

Griffen flushes in embarrassment, but at this point I'm almost immune to the cutting tone. Turning my gaze to the front, I see Beckett glaring at me.

"Sorry, professor."

His eyes darken, and last night's exchange races through my veins. Whatever my expression reveals compresses his lips in satisfaction. Then he spins toward the whiteboard.

"Pens out," he commands. "I want five hundred words on this topic. You have ten minutes."

Marker squeaks over the whiteboard, then drops with a clank. Beckett turns and sits, already opening a notebook and lifting a pen. At the low murmuring around me, I finally lift my gaze to the word on the board.

Orgasm.

I blink at it, waiting for a different word to appear. But I'm not that lucky. Not lucky at all, because when I glance down, Beckett is staring at me. One brow cocks in challenge.

So I write five hundred words about climbing a never-ending staircase to nowhere. When the ten minutes are up, I'm the first person he calls on. Of course. I read it to the class, earning chuckles from the women and speculative glances from the men.

Beckett is not amused but he hides it well, merely nodding and calling on another student. The next hours drag by in usual first-class format—introductions, lengthy discussion of the syllabus, and assignments of writing partners. There's an odd number in the class, and I'm in the last seat.

"She can join our group," offers Griffen.

Beckett's lips thin. "Ms. Eliot, you can submit your assignments to me for feedback."

My fellow students throw me sympathetic glances. I manage a smile and a nod, while inside I'm churning, feeling like a steel net is closing around me.

I can't escape him.

The final hour of class is a new lesson in endurance. Beckett speaks in depth about the first assignment—a fictional scene involving a couple who love each other but can't be together. The context, content, and style are completely up to us.

"Go ahead and enjoy leaving a few minutes early tonight," he says finally. "It's the last time it will happen."

As the room empties, I pack with purposeful slowness. The emotions on simmer since he first locked eyes on me boil over. I have to do something. *Now.* When the final student is gone, I stand and stalk to the front of the room.

"This has to stop," I say rigidly.

He glances up from his notebook. "What, exactly?"

"I can't concentrate," I snap. "Tone down the... whatever!"

His lips curl. "Eloquent, Ms. Eliot."

I groan, sinking fingers into the hair on my crown. "Look, Beckett. Beck. Whatever your name is. Last night was totally my fault. I completely lost my mind and forgot that you're my professor, my freaking *boss*. I'm not going to throw away the last two years of grad school on what you're hiding in your jeans. Whatever you may think, I'm not that kind of girl."

He blinks up at me. "I know. I finished your manuscript, by the way. Can you come to my office Monday after our morning class? I have a two-hour time block."

I stare at him and finally sputter, "It's like being in a blender. Every second, you make my head spin in a different direction. Is that your thing? You like targeting women, teasing them, baiting them, and watching them fall apart?"

He's around the desk so fast I only have time to gasp. Hot fingers grip the back of my bare neck, angling my face to his. His expression is an enticing mix of frustration and appeal.

"No," he whispers. "I don't know. Since you walked into class yesterday morning, I've been sideways over you. It doesn't make a lick of sense." Almost to himself, he adds, "Something about your eyes. Selkie-dark. So odd against your hair and skin."

The deepest, most damaged part of me roars to the surface and hijacks my voice. "Let's do it, then," I snarl. "Fuck me, and I guarantee you'll be over it. It's pretty much my M.O."

Shock drops his full lower lip. "Jesus, Iris, why would you say that?" he asks, scanning my eyes like he might find the answer in them.

I can't handle the intimacy of our stance and jerk away from his touch. Hastening to the back of the room, I grab my bag, then beeline for the door.

"Iris!" he snaps.

With my hand on the knob, I look at him. "The woman you were thinking about through the computer last night doesn't exist. Google my name, professor, and read about the accident. Maybe then we can get back to some semblance of a working relationship."

I wrench open the door and flee.

5. anti-hero

Over drinks at White Harp on Thursday night, I tell Claire everything. She listens with wide, unblinking eyes, her cocktail forgotten on the table. When I'm finished, I throw back a shot of whiskey and take a heavy swallow of my beer.

"I'm not sure what to say," she begins quietly. "On the one hand, good for you for throwing down the gauntlet. On the other, I kind of want to report him. You're his TA, for Christ's sake. Granted, he's only six years older than us and ridiculously attractive. So it's not skeevy or anything. But didn't he leave BU because of the same exact thing?"

"It's probably a fetish," I mutter.

"Why is he even here? He hasn't taught since BU,

and he churns out bestsellers like clockwork. It's not like he needs the cash."

I pinch the bridge of my nose. "I don't know. I think he really likes teaching. Or maybe he wants to redeem himself." Then I shake my head. "Who cares. He probably only got the job because the head of the graduate school is his buddy."

Claire takes a noisy slurp of her rum and coke. "This is nuts. Are you going to sleep with him?"

I gape at her. "What the fuck, Claire?"

She shrugs, grinning unrepentantly. "Exactly. Fuck. It will be good for you."

"Did you not hear a word I said? He's going to read about the accident and back off."

The laughter leaves her eyes. "Iris, listen. I've seen your scars. They're not as bad as you think. Have you ever considered that it's not the scars that makes boys—keyword *boys*—hightail it the next morning? Maybe your picker is broken."

I stare at my empty shot glass, unable to hold her gaze. "You think being the queen of one-night stands is a self-fulling prophecy."

She nods perfunctorily. "Face it, you never let the nice ones get close enough. Remember Brad? He was sweet as pie and half in love with you. You kept him in the friend zone so long I thought he'd Lady-of-Shallot himself."

I snort in spite of myself. "Good reference."

Claire grins. "Thanks, but are you hearing me? Brad knew about your scars and would have worshipped them because they were attached to you."

I lift a hand to stop her. "I'm not sure what that has to do with your advice to sleep with Beckett. He's on the opposite end of the spectrum from Brad."

She nods thoughtfully. "He is, but he's also opposite from all those dumb boys of our undergrad years. He's basically his own spectrum. He's worldly, obviously a deviant, and writes borderline-noir crime fiction. I bet he's going to be even more determined to have you. You're like the perfect tragic heroine."

I grimace even as her words elicit a shiver. "No way," I say weakly, scooting to the edge of the booth. "I'm going to the bar. You want another rum and coke?"

"Yep, thanks."

At the sight of the slammed counter, I pause in dismay. Without heels, I'm five-foot-five-inches of Never Going to Get a Drink. I almost return to beg Claire to go, but in my final sweep I spot a familiar figure sitting on a barstool.

I squeeze past four frat boys lost on their way to

Greek Row and tap the man's shoulder. As angry voices rise behind me, Griffen turns.

"Iris! Hey." He gives me a one-arm hug and glares over my shoulder. As he looks like a cowboy who can wrestle bulls without breaking a sweat, the muttering instantly fades.

"Thank you," I say, hopping onto the brass rail near the floor. I wave down the bartender and once my order is taken, turn to face Griffen.

"Are you here alone?" I ask curiously.

He nods. "Stood up, apparently," he says, chuckling. "Ah, well, there's enough familiar faces around that I don't feel like too much of a loser."

"You're not," I assure him.

He winks and takes a pull from his bottle. "Beckett's really got it out for you, huh? Aren't you TA for his undergrad course, too?"

"Yep," I say, smiling thinly. "I think I get on his nerves."

"Yeah, you're a regular pain in the ass," he quips, "fucking up the bell curve for the last two years."

I laugh and shove his shoulder, which is like pushing a brick wall. "Whatever, your GPA was higher than mine last year."

He grins. "Damn straight. I have my eye on a PhD."

My drinks arrive and I add them to our tab. "If you get bored, come hang out with Claire and me."

His focus sharpens. "Claire? That's your roommate, right? Tall brunette?"

I laugh. "Sorry, buddy, she's taken."

"How taken?"

I think of Monty, whose definition of romance is reading Descartes aloud while Claire cooks him dinner. "Fifty to sixty percent."

Griffen immediately stands, leaving his empty beer on the counter. "I like those odds."

Laughing, I hand him Claire's and my drinks. "Back right, corner booth. I'm going to use the ladies room. See you in a minute."

"Make it ten," he says, winking as he strolls toward my roommate.

Feeling like a naughty fairy godmother—who's going to get an earful on the walk home—I skirt around the bar crowd. I'm several steps away from the back hallway when I hear Beckett's name. It's spoken in a pleading tone by a female voice, and my eyes wander until I find her in a nearby booth.

Sitting with her—practically *under* her—is the man himself.

"Come *on*," whines the woman, who I recognize vaguely from campus. "Let's get out of here!"

Some evil convergence of acoustics brings me his soft words. "If you're that anxious, Maggie, just unbutton your pants a bit. I'll take care of you right here."

"Beck!" she squeals.

I make a sound—a coughing gag, or a gagging wheeze, or something equally indicative of revulsion—and jerk into motion again.

Grateful for the alcohol-induced buffer between my brain and the odd thrum of pain in my chest, I wait in the short line, take care of business, and hurry back toward the promise of more alcohol.

I'm halfway to our table when someone grabs my arm. My momentum carries me full around and against a familiar leather jacket. Gasping, I look up at Beckett. His other hand curls around my hip, holding me against him as I try to squirm away.

"Stop moving," he growls.

"Let me go," I retort, lifting my chin and meeting his burning eyes. "There are students and faculty all around us."

Like I just told him I'm a leper, his touch vanishes. But his eyes stay locked on my face, searing and full of... *anger?*

"What the hell is wrong with you?" I hiss, glancing around to make sure we're not being observed.

The anger, too, vanishes. "I'm incredibly sorry that happened to you," he says.

The accident.

I twitch a shoulder. "Great. Does this mean we can act normally now?"

"If you're asking whether I still want to fuck you silly, the answer is yes. Because apparently that's my normal setting where you're concerned."

My heart rate spikes, fire raging through my limbs. "You can't say stuff like that!"

His gaze roams my face. "Come home with me, Iris. Right now."

I shake my head, choking on hysterical laughter. "You're seriously deranged. I'm not sleeping with you! I've known you less than a week, and you're my *professor*."

"Beck, darling? Who are you talking to?" It's the chirping voice from earlier, which belongs to the woman whose arms are now wrapping around his torso. She peers around his shoulder at me. "Oh, hello. You're James' TA, aren't you?"

James.

The alcohol turns in my stomach. Annoyance and embarrassment tighten Beckett's features; he remembers as well as I do his words from last night. That once I slept with him, I could call him James.

You're disgusting, I tell him with my eyes.

"Yep. Just saying hello." By some miracle, my voice comes out normal. Polite, even. "See you Monday, professor."

I make it back to the booth, but after five minutes of listening to Griffen do his damnedest to charm Claire, I mumble excuses and grab my coat.

"It's pretty late," says Claire worriedly. "Do you want us to walk you home?"

Behind me, a British piece of shit says, "I'll drive her home."

"Professor Beckett, nice to see you," says Griffen, surprise twinned with uncertainty. He looks questioningly at me.

Synapses fire at lightning speed as I weigh my options and realize there's only one that doesn't make this situation even more suspect. Clenching my teeth, I turn and look up at Beckett.

"Thanks so much, I'd really appreciate that."

His lips twitch, and he gives Claire and Griffen a short nod. "Enjoy your evening." With a hand on my lower back, he guides me from the pub.

The second we're outside, I move away from him. "My apartment isn't far. Thanks for the offer, though!"

A block later, he joins me as I wait for the crosswalk. As Thursday night is a pretty big party night, we're surrounded by people. Most of them are drunk or high and not paying attention to us, but we're definitely not in private. Which is why when deft fingers stroke my hair back from my temple, I don't start screaming at him.

"Soft as it looks," he murmurs.

"Go back to your conquest, professor," I whisper scathingly.

His head bends near my ear. "Have you always been this fiery, or do I merely bring out the best in you?"

I squeeze my eyes shut. "You've got to be kidding me." Turning toward him, I poke him in the chest and glare into his laughing eyes. "You just finger fucked a woman in a White Harp booth, and now you want to take me home? Not happening!"

He blinks. "I—what? I absolutely did not."

"You said, and I quote, 'just unbutton your pants a bit and I'll take care of you right here.'"

He throws back his head and laughs. "If you must know, little eavesdropper, I was calling her bluff. Maggie fancied herself a walk on the wild side but when push came to shove, she caved."

I stare at him, mouth opening and closing. "I don't... you're—"

He grins rakishly. "A prick, yes. We've already determined this. What I want to know, Iris, is whether you have the guts to take me on."

The crosswalk finally chirps—*thank you, universe*—and saves me from a response. I escape, running into the camouflage of the thick pedestrian flow. Despite the fiery protest of my knee, I don't stop running until my building is in sight. Taking the steps two at a time, I burst into the lobby and jab the button for the elevator.

My veins are live wires, twitching my legs and feet, and every few seconds I glance toward the front doors.

No Beckett.

The elevator opens and I rush inside.

6. archetype

Maybe Claire's right, and the scars aren't as bad as I think. They're eleven years old, after all, most of them faded nearly white. But the roots of tragedies like mine sink deep into the psyche, a virus designed especially for the cracks of broken hearts.

My scars are daily reminders, just like the ache in my knee when I overexert myself or when the weather drops below a certain temperature. *Derrick is dead. Because of you, he's dead.* There's no escaping the truth. The recurring nightmares. The moments when reality breaks apart and I think I see him in a crowd. Or I hear a laugh that sounds exactly like his.

The writer and theologian Frederick Buechner said, *'Here is the world. Beautiful and terrible things will happen. Don't be afraid.'*

He's partly right. There's beauty here, and terrible things certainly happen. In some form or another, tragedy strikes everyone at least once in their lives. An illness, a death, violence, a natural disaster... I've yet to meet someone who's been spared. I hope that most, however, will never have to live through what I have. That they'll never have to learn the lesson that fear is sometimes all that saves you.

When the memories are particularly bad, I call my mom and tell her. The same disease lives inside her—the disease of tragedy that forever atrophies a portion of your heart. But these days, it's harder for us to reach that place of commiseration. She's been in therapy for a long time. Eight years ago, she fell in love with a nice man and got married. I have two stepsisters now, one of them still in high school. My mother is busy raising her, being an adored wife, and teaching dance to toddlers. Pursuing happiness. Like she should.

Like I should.

Monday morning, I stare at my reflection the bathroom mirror and say, "I'm happy." My eyes—*selkie-dark*, he called them—are squinted with skepticism. "Happiness is a frame of mind. A choice. Today I will be happy."

The affirmations work most of the time, temporary psychological bandaids on my brokenness. Today, not so much. I feel fractured and odd. Having slept on damp hair, the white-blonde strands are wavy and haphazard. I consider a bun, but the weather has taken a turn and my ears need the warmth.

Claire, who's put up with my sullenness all weekend, hands me a thermos of coffee when I walk into the kitchen.

"Bless you," I say, tucking it under my arm as I yank on gloves.

She peers into my face. "Did you have a nightmare last night?" I nod, and she clucks in sympathy. "Anything I can do?"

I smirk tiredly. "Dump Monty and go out with Griffen."

A blush blooms on her cheeks and she laughs. "You're merciless. I thought you liked Monty."

I shrug. "There's nothing wrong with him, per se. But more importantly, do *you* like him?"

She purses her lips. "He's really nice and super smart."

I point at her face. "That look, right there. The faintly irritated one you get around him. That's why I sent you sexy cowboy bait."

She snorts, turning to gather her bag and thermos, then joins me at the door. We take the elevator down in silence, lift the hoods of our raincoats as we walk across the lobby, then step into the grey world of drizzle.

Not until we're waiting among other students at the crosswalk leading onto campus do I make my final move.

"You've been dating Monty, what, four months now?"

"About that, yeah."

"Did you forget our bedrooms share a wall?"

She shoots me a frown. "What's your point?"

I smile sweetly. "Claire-bear, I know what it sounds like when you're being taken care of. And it's not happening."

She screws her eyes shut. "Damnit. It's so not."

I laugh, linking my arm with hers as the crosswalk opens. Once on campus, we part ways in the middle of the massive central plaza. Before she's out of earshot, I cup hands around my mouth and shout, "Just think about what I said!"

She doesn't turn, merely extending a gloved middle finger over her head. Chuckling to myself, I head to class.

I'm sufficiently early today. To my relief, the head desk is empty when I walk into the room. Several students look up from their phones, smiling in greeting.

"How'd the homework go, guys?" I ask, perching on an empty desk.

Janice groans. "Five revisions, and I have no idea whether or not it's absolute crap. And my journaling was horrible. I kept forgetting to do it."

Terrence—of the infected nose ring metaphor—grunts in empathy. "The first assignments are always the worst because every professor grades differently." He looks curiously at me. "Do you think he'll do the grading or hand everything off to you?"

"I'm not sure," I hedge, "but don't assume I'll have a lighter touch than Professor Beckett."

He winces. "Oh, I know. Whenever I've had a TA grade my work, they've been brutal."

I laugh. "It's a rite of passage. The chain of student suffering."

Molly, the mousey brunette who I know has a massive crush on Beckett, coughs lightly. "I didn't think the assignment was that hard. And daily journaling is an integral part of maintaining and growing your craft."

"Good perspective, Molly," I reply, although I don't necessarily agree. "I'm glad you're already getting something out of it."

More students enter the room. I abandon my perch for my desk in back, draping my damp coat over the chair to dry. As the clock hits 9:03, then 9:07 with no Beckett, I pull out my phone to see if I've missed an email from him. No email, but there's a text from an out-of-state number.

Late

"Ya think?" I mutter, then put my phone away and walk to the front of class. "Professor Beckett is running late, so let's go ahead and start. Assignments and journals to the front, please. Good idea, Greg—everyone, tuck your short story proposals into the front of the journals. Thanks."

Good-natured grumbling commences as papers rustle and basic composition notebooks are passed up the rows. I collect the journals and place them on the desk, then lean back and cross my arms in an unconscious mirroring of Beckett.

"Let's talk about your short stories. You were supposed to deliver at least one character profile as well as a rough outline. Any issues?"

"Thinking of an idea that didn't suck," mumbles Greg, and several students laugh.

"It's not easy, is it?" I ask, nodding. "Did anyone have success with my suggestion to spend some quiet time daydreaming?"

Molly raises her hand. "I did. It really helped, especially thinking about people in my life who are interesting or have some mystery about them." Her face turns slowly red and she bows her head.

At a commotion outside the door, we all turn. Through the small window, we have the misfortune of seeing Beckett kissing a woman—Maggie from the bar. An elbow hits the door, and I hear his low laughter. After some soft murmurs, they say goodbye and Beckett strolls into the room.

"Morning!" he chirps, pulling off his coat. "Thanks, Ms. Eliot, I'll take it from here."

I walk to my desk, hoping my stiff movements and frozen face go unnoticed.

"Sorry for my tardiness, class," he says breezily. "Something came up."

The men snicker, the women blush, and I stare fixedly at my clenched, bloodless hands. Emotions clog my airways—disgust, anger, and delayed embarrassment for the computer-chat incident. There's hurt, too, and a small, poisonous green flame of jealousy.

Damn him.

As Beckett launches into a lecture and discussion on the three short stories students were required to read since last week, I devote myself to beginning an assignment for another class. It's my final poetry course, thankfully taught by one of my favorite professors.

Beckett's voice fades to the background, becoming a tolerable irritant as I play with couplets. The remainder of the period flies. When desks scrape on the floor, I look up to find the classroom emptying.

At the front, Beckett sits at his desk, writing something in his ever-present notebook. Wanting to escape before he can speak to me, I hurriedly gather my things and lift my coat from the chair.

"Wait, Ms. Eliot."

So close.

Giving the door a final, longing glance, I turn to face him. "Yes?"

He glances up—a virescent flash—then back down. "I need to cancel our meeting today."

I'd completely forgotten about it. "Okay, no problem," I say, not bothering to hide my relief.

Pen dropping, he stretches backward with a groan, lacing fingers behind his head. I drop my gaze quickly from the alluring sight.

"How was your weekend?" he asks mildly.

My eyes snap to his smiling face. "Great," I grind out. "How was yours?"

"Superb."

"Fabulous. Anything else?"

His smile sharpens. "Yes, actually. I need you to grade these." He waves a hand at the stack of fourteen notebooks.

My stomach sinking, I nod and walk forward. "I'll have them ready for next week's class."

"Nope. By Thursday's workshop."

"You're joking!"

"Not at all."

I grip the edge of his desk, staring down at him with naked annoyance. "Is this punishment? For not bending over for you?"

His gaze meanders down my body. "Interesting choice of words, Ms. Eliot, but with you I'd prefer face to face."

My cheeks flame and my brains trips to red.

"That's it," I snap. "I quit."

Spinning away, I storm to the door and yank it open. Beckett's hand over my head slams it shut. I tug ineffectually on the handle, throwing all my weight into it, but he merely lifts his other palm to the door.

With a cry of frustration, I turn and shove him back. He barely moves, chuckling as I try for the handle again.

"Why on Earth do I enjoy pissing you off so much?" he asks lightly. "It's become my favorite hobby."

"Because you're an asshole," I growl. Giving up, I spin and drop my forehead to the cool door. "This is sexual harassment. I should report you."

There's a weighted pause. "Perhaps you should, but

you won't. You're not going to quit, or report me, because you like how I make you feel."

"You don't know me," I say helplessly.

"I want to. Very much."

I feel him behind me, close enough that heat radiates onto my back. His breath whispers through my hair.

"Don't think I can't see my effect on you, and never doubt your effect on me. In my experience, attraction like this doesn't happen often. Once or twice in a life-time, if we're lucky. I've tried very hard to ignore it, but when I see you something... changes in me."

His words pour through me, driving blood low in my body. To the place that screams for what only he can give. But regardless of how badly I want what he's offering, I'm not naive enough to fall for his poet's tongue.

"Is that what you said to Maggie? And however many countless others you've cleaved through like a wheat field?"

"Mmm, pleasant analogy, pet, but I as a rule I don't lie to women I'm courting. Maggie only bothers you because she's tasted what you want."

He's right—and I hate him for it.

Turning until my spine is against the door, I look up at him. His eyes are soft, unguarded and direct. It almost buckles me, but not quite.

"I'm not a shiny toy, Beckett. You seem to have made

it to adulthood without learning the lesson that we don't always get what we want."

His eyes cloud. "On the contrary, I know that lesson well." His thumb swipes over my hot cheek and across my temple, fingers sinking into my loose hair. In his usual quicksilver way, he changes topics. "You write beautifully, Iris. Raw and elegant, with astounding depth. I'm absolutely floored by you."

I'm unraveling, made defenseless by the words, the sudden vulnerability of his expression. If he asked for me now, this instant, I'd give myself wholeheartedly and damn the consequences.

But he doesn't, saying instead, "Forgive me." He looks away, hand falling and jaw clenching, then steps back and walks toward his desk. "Before reading your manuscript, I thought..." He shakes his head. "You're right to deny me."

Survival instinct takes over before I ask what the hell he means.

"Are you saying you'll stop?"

"Teasing you, arousing you, maddening you? I can't promise that, but I'll do my best." And then, because he's brilliant and perceptive, he answers my unspoken question. "You're not a casual fuck, and I don't date. If I did..." he sighs, "I'd probably quit this bloody job for a shot at making you mine. But you need a better man than me, Iris."

My ears ring with his pronouncement. I have no idea what to say, how to feel. Nothing makes sense. I feel like I'm dreaming, or falling, or caught in an undertow.

Words spill unbidden from that dark place inside me. "What if you're wrong, and I don't want to date?"

His head lifts, eyes narrowing. "Iris..." he warns.

Oh my God, what am I doing?

But the need is too great, and I'm powerless over it. "I'm scarred, Beckett. I'm not one of your perfect girls. What if all I want is an experienced man to make me feel beautiful again? Can you do that, or will you hide revulsion and run at first chance?"

He draws a swift breath, eyes darkening as his pupils expand. I've never seen anything more enthralling.

I did that to him.

"I'm not afraid of scars, and perfect is in the eye of the beholder. I already know you are. Every inch of you."

We're ten feet apart, but it feels like an electric chord snaps taut between us. Thick and pulsing, no wishful thinking will break it. Or change it.

"This is inevitable, isn't it?" I whisper.

He nods shortly; I see his fingers clench on the edge of the desk. "What are you doing Friday night?"

I take the plunge. "You."

Eyes closing briefly, something like relief crosses his face. "Thank God." A wicked smile overtakes his mouth. "Don't think this means you're getting out of grading."

The tension shivers down to manageable levels. I walk forward and gather the journals. A safe three feet of desk between us, I meet his victorious eyes.

"You're a supercilious prick, Beckett."

He bites his lip on a cheeky grin. "In four days, this prick is all yours."

My face heats, but I rally and glance down meaningfully. "Looks like you need to cool off."

Purposefully misinterpreting me, he says, "While we... engaged, there won't be anyone else."

I nod. "Good. I want your undivided attention. Repeatedly."

He rolls his eyes in aggravation. "Stop, please. Good God. I have to leave this room eventually, you know." I giggle, then slap a hand over my mouth in embarrassment. He just grins at me, eyes almost iridescent with delight. "Glad to know my discomfort amuses you. Now scram."

"Yes, professor," I say sweetly, and he groans, sinking dramatically into the chair with his fingers clenched on his head.

As I head to my small, shared office with arms full of

journals and a stupid smile on my face, I think about what just happened. What's going to happen. What it will feel like to have all his skill and passion unleashed on me. His body inside mine.

And for the first time in a long time, I forget my pain, my guilt and brokenness, and enjoy the simple surrender of anticipation.

By some miracle of the graduate student gods, I finish grading by Wednesday afternoon, leaving me just enough time to proofread and polish the assignment due for Beckett's class.

Written late last night, my scene is a lurid imaginary chapter in the lives of two women, both married to men, who've loved each other since they were girls. The finished product is a lot more depressing than I'd originally intended, but I think it's pretty poignant.

I hope he likes it.

It's raining in earnest as I hustle through the stormy night. For the millionth time in two years, I bemoan the fact our apartment is on the west side of campus, the furthest possible location from the English Department. Claire fairs slightly better, though she still has a substantial trek. Nevertheless, our two-bedroom unit is a prized commodity: close to campus, spacious, with high-ceilings, wood floors, and two masters. There's no way we'd give it up.

Licking wind-driven raindrops from my lips, I tell myself repeatedly that walking is good for my knee. Good for my knee or not, by the time I reach class I'm limping. Not looking toward the front of the room, I lower myself carefully into the seat next to Griffen.

"You okay, Iris?" he asks softly.

I realize my face is scrunched in pain and forcefully relax my expression. "Yeah, just an old injury. Swift weather change makes it act up."

Griffen leans a little closer, lowering his voice. "Beckett seems in a much better mood tonight. He was even whistling a minute ago."

My lips twitching involuntarily, I allow myself a peek. When I find Beckett already watching me, my heart gives a heavy thump. His expression, however, isn't anything I was expecting—he looks downright worried. His gaze flickers to my desk, then back up, eyebrows drawing together.

He mouths, *Your knee?*

Flushing with misplaced humiliation, I nod shortly and duck my head.

"What was that about?" whispers Griffen.

Cursing the ingrained voyeurism of writers, I think fast. "I sent him an email mentioning I might be late because of the long walk and my bad knee. He was just asking if I was okay."

Griffen's gaze is heavy on my face. "That was nice of him. Glad you two have buried the hatchet."

By force of will, I don't physically react to the unintentional innuendo, and I'm saved a response as Beckett stands to signal the beginning of class.

Pain makes the first hour and a half feel like ten. At the midway break, all I have energy for is dropping my head to my desk. Students leave to stretch their legs, grab coffee or a smoke, and check their phones. Griffen offers to bring me ibuprofen, and I gladly accept.

When the room goes quiet, I hear footsteps, then smell a mouthwatering trace of Beckett's cologne. Cracking my eyes open, I watch him crouch beside my desk and fold his arms next to mine.

"You're in a lot of pain," he says softly. "Can Claire come pick you up?"

"We don't have cars."

"Then can I get you anything? Ice? How about another chair so you can extend your leg?"

"I'm fine, thanks," I say, but pain embitters the words. Sitting up, I make sure the room is empty. "You're too close right now. It's making me crazy."

As I'd hoped, the words sweep away his worry. One of his arms drops beneath the desk, a smile flirting with his lips. Seconds later, fingers trail up my thigh. Gasping, I seize his hand before it can go further.

I give the door a wide-eyed glance. *"Beckett."*

"What? I'm checking in on a student who's in obvious discomfort." As he speaks, he teases our fingers together, then guides my unresisting hand toward my lap. Once at the seam of my jeans, he angles our knuckles and drags them slowly downward.

Everything in the world narrows to the sensations in my body and the green of his eyes. For the first time, I notice tiny flecks of yellow and blue in them.

"My God," he whispers hoarsely, "your face right now. You're a fucking vision."

Laughter nears the door. Before I can fully process the threat of discovery, Beckett is gone, striding to his desk and sliding quickly behind it. I drop my head back down, burying my face in my arms and praying for my pulse to slow.

"Here you go, Iris," says Griffen.

I sit up to accept a bottle of water and a packet of pain pills. "Thanks so much, what do I owe you?"

"On the house," he says with a wink. "Claire texted me today."

My mouth opens in surprise. "Hallelujah!"

He laughs. "I take it you weren't a fan of her ex?"

"Ex?" I repeat, then punch his shoulder. "Did she say she broke up with him? I haven't seen her since this morning."

He nods, grinning. "Guess I made the right first impression."

"I'll say. Way to go, champ."

He chuckles. "You seem like you're feeling better. Pain let up?"

The pain is still there, but its ache is secondary now to the one between my legs. My eyes flicker to Beckett, currently writing in his notebook. I watch his hand moving and have a vivid fantasy of that same rhythm applied elsewhere.

"Um, yeah," I say belatedly. "I'm feeling better, thanks."

Griffen, who's too damned smart for his own good, gives me a probing look. "Iris, are you crushing on Beckett?"

"No!" I say.

Too quickly. Too loudly.

Griffen's brows go up, a huge grin on his face. "Holy Smokes, you are!"

Realizing I just stepped in a shitpile, I take the only reasonable way out. "Okay, so I am. But he, uh, told me

I'm not his type. Don't tell anyone, seriously, it's so embarrassing."

Griffen hoots and slaps his desk.

A few rows up, Kirk turns around. "What's so funny back there?"

Griffen sobers, but his lips curve mischievously. "Iris needs a boyfriend," he says brightly. "Badly."

Ah, fuck.

The whole class, back now that break is almost over, turns to stare at me. I wheeze and elbow Griffen.

"Ha Ha, he's just kidding."

"You're single, Iris?" asks Meredith, a statuesque blonde with the rare combination of brains and beauty. "Come out with me this weekend. We'll find you a good one!"

Kirk raises his hand. "Can I volunteer?"

"Alright, people," snaps Beckett. "Ms. Eliot's love life is no longer a topic of concern. Your dismal display of reading comprehension, however, is very much concerning..."

After a second lecture, writing exercise, and finally, submission of our narratives, my brain feels like sandpaper and I can barely keep my eyes open. It's nearing ten o'clock, and a glance outside confirms that the rain is now coming down in sheets.

My knee is mostly recovered and only twinges a little as I stand and experiment with weight. Griffen accompanies me down the hallway, pausing when I stop near the elevator.

"Are you sure you can walk home?"

I nod. "Been doing it for years. Thanks for the concern, though. You're a sweetheart. I'm glad you hit it off with Claire."

He smiles. "Me too. See you later."

He disappears down the stairs and by the time I reach ground level, he's gone. The building itself is a graveyard, empty but for a janitor. Steeling myself, I flex my knee a little, then pull up my hood and walk toward the doors.

"Iris!"

I stop, poised between dark rain and dry light, to see Beckett running agilely down the stairs. Watching him move gives me a fuzzy feeling in my gut. The power and grace in his limbs, his lean virility—it's intoxicating.

He stops before me, breathing lightly. "I took a bus today because my car's in the shop, but please let me walk you home. It's late and pouring. Please."

I blink in bemusement; that warm feeling intensifies. "Are you that worried for my safety?"

He doesn't hesitate. "Yes. Let me walk you home."

I nod. "But just so we're clear, I'm not inviting you in."

"I know." He glances outside. "Just so we're clear, if you trip I get to carry you."

My brows lift. "What happens if you trip?"

He chuckles. "I won't. Come on." With a final glance into the building, he ushers me into the rain.

The first impact makes us both flinch, but after several minutes of exposure the deluge resolves into a portal to another world. A beautiful one, filled with blurred scenery and the dull roar of driving wind and rain.

There's no way to keep our faces and hair from being soaked, and boots can only do so much. The most important items, at least, are safe in bags beneath our jackets.

By the time we're halfway across the central plaza, I'm limping again. Beckett notices immediately, snaking an arm around my waist to offer support. I let him give it, because the icy heat in my knee is now flowing up to my hip.

"Let's stop for a minute," he says.

I nod and give in to temptation, curling into his chest and leaning heavily against him. His arms come around me, sheltering me as best he can. Despite our thick coats and the messenger bags beneath them, we fit. Just like I knew we would.

The steady rain lulls me into a peaceful stasis, one in which it makes perfect sense to lift my face, brushing my cheek along his jaw. Like poetry, his face turns and his rain-wet lips find mine. He kisses me gently at first, reverently. Then, as I open for him, he angles his head to devour my offering.

The first taste of his tongue is ambrosia. Shuddering, I reach my hands beneath his hood to grab his wet hair and pull him closer. I feel the vibration in his chest as he groans.

When we break apart to catch our breath, he murmurs, "As far as first kisses go, that rewrote the book."

I nod dazedly. The necessary separation of our bodies, coupled with the relentless pounding of the rain, gave a singular gravity to the moment. It was beyond perfect, like no kiss I've had before. And for some reason, the acknowledgment sends a shiver of disquiet through me.

I hide my confusion with a smirk. "We might as well stop there. I'm not sure we can be beat that."

He smiles, a finger drawing across my tingling lower lip. "Oh ye of little faith."

I make a show of glancing skyward and his hand drops away. "Look at that, the rain is letting up."

"Mmm, yes, look at that," he says dryly.

I step back, adjusting my coat to avoid his eyes. "I can make it from here. Thanks."

"Iris?" The tone is soft, uncertain. "What's going on in your head?"

I force a smile. "Nothing. Just tired." Several small groups of students move in our direction, taking advantage of the paused downpour. As they draw nearer, I add lightly, "You should go. Avoid that rumor mill."

He glances at the approaching group and sighs. "Will you text me when you make it home, at least?"

"Yes. Good night, Beckett."

I turn and limp away, and almost don't hear his whispered correction. "James."

8. aubade

Friday afternoon after my office hours and poetry class, I catch a bus to meet Claire for a late lunch in Fremont. The weather is frigid but clear, another storm not due until Sunday.

When I arrive at our favorite artsy café, Tullamore, it's slammed, no tables or chairs in sight. I don't see Claire, so I head outside to call her. She answers on the first ring.

"I'm on the back patio. The heaters are on so it's habitable. Is the wait still long?"

I make my way back inside to join the line. "It's not bad. Keep the table. What do you want?"

She rattles off an order and we hang up. The line moves quickly, the staff efficient as always. Before five minutes pass, I'm at the counter.

"Hi, what can I get you?" asks a slim, lovely brunette with amazing curls. She looks familiar, but I can't place where I know her from.

"Two large lattes and two turkey-avocado sandwiches, please."

"Sure thing." She jots down the order and shouts at the barista, who nods. "Anything else?"

"Nope, thanks." As she takes my money, I can't help asking, "Do we know each other?"

She gives me a searching look, then visibly brightens. "You're Allison's sister, right? Sorry, I forgot your name."

It clicks when I spy her name tag. *Rose.* "I think we met at Allison's last year. I'm Iris."

"That's right, we're the flower girls!" she says, grinning. She glances meaningfully over my shoulder. "I'd totally chat, but the line is getting out of hand again."

"Oops, sorry." Blushing, I grab the table placard she's offering and move away from the register.

"Great to see you, Iris!"

"You, too!" I call, then head down the hallway and outside.

Claire looks up from a book, smile faltering as she sees me. "What's wrong?"

I shake my head. "Nothing. I'm just super awkward in public."

She laughs. "You just described every grad student I know."

I share her laughter. "True story. What are you reading?" With a sheepish grin, she shows me the cover. My mouth drops. "'*When a Cowboy Comes Calling*'? Are you serious with this right now?"

She snorts and tosses the trashy romance to the table. "It's your fault. I finally saw the light and ended things with Monty. Now I'm in lust with Griffen." Her expression becomes vulnerable. "He's a good guy, right?"

"Yes," I say honestly. "He's respectful, hardworking, and his GPA is higher than mine. He's also funny, kind, and *hello*, he's a real-life cowboy."

She grins in relief. "Okay. Well, I guess I'm moving to Texas next year."

We're still giggling when our food and drinks arrive. Surprisingly, they're delivered by Rose.

"Hey, Iris, sorry I didn't recognize you earlier," she says, smiling sweetly. "My brain is totally on the fritz. I've, uh, developed a *thing* about people asking if they know me."

Although I don't actually know her outside our one meeting and through random intel from Allison, another vague memory surfaces.

"Oh, are you still, um, dealing with fallout from

that…" I rack my brain and can't for the life of me remember.

Rose grins. "I gotta say, it's pretty awesome you have no idea."

Claire coughs over the words, "*Breaking Giants.*"

At mention of the wildly popular band, a lightbulb flashes. "Oh—right."

Rose laughs, but it's impossible to miss the sadness that clouds her eyes. Glancing between Claire and me, she asks softly, "Have you ever met someone who just… fits you? Only there's twenty million obstacles in the way?"

"Yes," I whisper.

Her eyes narrow on me, her voice lowering with sudden intensity. "Whatever you do, don't sleep with him, Iris. Unless he's ready to be the man you need. I mean it. Worst seven-hour mistake ever."

Words fail me, so I just nod.

Claire chokes softly on her coffee. "Seven hours?" she squeaks.

Rose looks away, smiling faintly, but her eyes stay sad. After a moment, she shakes her head and stands. "God, I'm such a downer. Sorry ladies." Bending, she gives me an unexpected kiss on the cheek. "Nice to see you, Iris. You should call Allison more. I know you're step-siblings and whatnot, but she loves you."

With a wave, she disappears inside.

Claire whistles softly. "I have no idea if she was talking about Matt Sullivan or Julian Ashburn, but *seven hours?* How could seven hours with one of them be a mistake?"

"I don't know," I say, while privately, thinking of Beckett, I admit, *Very easily.*

Like the man has ESP, my phone buzzes on the table. I look down, read the text, then close my eyes. I've been ignoring his calls and all emails except ones pertaining to class.

You're backing out, aren't you?

"Who was that?" asks Claire.

I take an unsteady breath. "No one."

———

A house party is exactly where I don't want to be on a Friday night. Especially *this* Friday. But Griffen invited Claire, and she begged me to be the third wheel. The prospect of doing homework alone in my room while fighting the urge to call Beckett is dismal enough that I don't complain. Not out loud, at least.

The crowd is mostly grad students, and they mesh for a humorous blend of nearly incomprehensible, high-brow conversations and scandalous antics. Techno music blares from huge speakers in the cleared out living room, and at least twenty bodies are gyrating beneath a tired disco ball. Women cluster together with flirting eyes, while men make asses of themselves to score the hottest dance partner.

I'm sitting on a plastic folding chair near the front door, and my greatest enjoyment in the last hour has been the cold gusts of air every time it opens. That, and the flask in my hand.

Claire disappeared twenty minutes ago with Griffen. I'm just drunk enough to be jealous. Griffen is so *nice*, and he's clearly a steady, capable man. One who wants to date. Learn about his partner. Maybe, eventually, think about long term.

Basically the opposite of James Beckett.

"Iris?"

I look up and recognize Kirk. "How's it going?" I yell over the music.

"Good, good. I'm surprised to see you here!" He bobs his head, hips jerking to the beat. Off-rhythm, unfortunately. Bending down, he yells in the direction of my ear, "Wanna dance?"

I lean back so his beer breath doesn't make me gag. "No, thanks! Bad knee!"

"Ah, that sucks," he says, gaze bouncing around

nervously. He drags his free hand through brown hair very much in need of a trim.

Ashamed of my critical thoughts, I point to the empty chair next to me. "Sit down!"

He blinks in surprise, then smiles like I just offered to kiss him. Dropping his lanky body beside me, I immediately regret my decision. He smells like a bottle of cheap cologne.

I'm too old for this shit.

Leaning toward me again, he asks, "So, what's it like being Beckett's TA? He scares the crap out of me! Have you read his books? He's brilliant!"

I muster a smile. "He's a tyrant, but yeah, he's a great writer."

"Has he hit on you yet? I heard that's his thing. I saw him last week coming out of his office with some woman." He laughs loudly. "She was *tore up from the floor up*, if you know what I mean!"

My stomach turns. "Dear God," I mutter, sending the plea to the spinning disco ball. With a meaningful glance at my watch, I stand up and point toward the back of the house. "I'm going to find my friend. Nice talking to you, Kirk!"

Too drunk to notice the brush off, he bobs his head amicably. "See you Wednesday!"

I walk through the living room with its miniature

orgy and into the packed kitchen. On the other side of an island filled with half-empty bottles of booze, I see Claire with her tongue down Griffen's throat.

Raising my flask in silent salute, I drain its contents. Beside me, a man lifts a bottle of vodka in my direction. "Refill?" he asks, grinning.

"Nope, thanks." Although I'm not adverse to the idea of more alcohol, at parties such as this one I never drink anything from bottles I don't personally see opened.

Within seconds, someone else offers me another drink, this time from an unmarked red cup. I shake my head and quickly head back the way I came, then straight out the front door. As soon as it closes behind me, I feel better. And worse, because Griffen was my ride home.

"Iris, is that you?" asks Meredith the Statuesque, coming up the front steps with two girlfriends in toe.

"It's me," I agree, sitting heavily on the top step.

Meredith sends her friends inside and perches beside me. "You okay?"

I laugh, then realize I sound like a lunatic. "Sorry," I say quickly. "I'm fine. Just boy problems."

She rolls her eyes skyward. "I hear that. What's going on?"

I shrug. "He wants a physical-only sort of thing, and I'm not sure I can handle it."

She makes a noise of sympathy. "Do you have feelings for him?"

"Define feelings," I say morosely. "I can tell you he makes me crazy. Most of the time I don't know whether to slap him or kiss him."

Meredith grins. "Sounds passionate. Have you slept with him?"

The odd magic of college parties, I muse, is having frankly intimate conversations with almost-strangers. "Nope. I'm afraid if I do, I'll get attached. He's..." I shrug, "pretty amazing."

She nudges my shoulder with hers. "I guess you have to decide if your fear of the unknown is greater than your desire to be close to him."

I blink at her as the words sink through me, stirring up a dangerous conviction. My desire to be close to James Beckett.

"I really wish you hadn't said that," I finally say.

She frowns. "Why?" I pull my phone out of my pocket and she laughs, standing. With a final squeeze of my shoulder, she says, "Good luck, buttercup," and heads inside.

Chin up, buttercup. Come out swinging.

Fate or accident, Meredith's words trigger memory

of my brother's voice. I have no idea what it portends, but I scroll through the contacts on my phone with new determination. I find *Beckett* and hit Send.

It rings three times.

"Iris?" A pause. "Where are you?"

I tell him the nearest cross street. "Come get me, James."

He draws a breath. "I'll be there in ten minutes."

I hang up, send a text to Claire letting her know I found a ride, and make my way down the street to the corner. It's dark and cold, my wool coat barely sufficient to keep the chill from my bones.

As the minutes pass, my nerve falters countless times. I wish I had more alcohol—I wish I wasn't so buzzed. I wish I had on nicer underwear, a lace bra. Perfume.

Did I shave my legs this morning?

"Oh fuck," I mutter, rubbing my cold face with my hands.

Just as I reach peak anxiety, a car pulls up in front of me. The driver's door opens and closes. Before I even look, I know it's him. I can feel him getting closer like an asteroid on collision course.

"Iris, look at me."

I lower my hands. Beckett scans my face, then his gaze flickers to the flask peeking from my coat pocket.

"You've been drinking," he says mildly.

"Yes. Bourbon."

His lips curl. "I'm either impressed or disappointed, hard to say." A hesitation. "Shall I take you home?"

Fire surges in my blood. "Do you want me or not?"

He takes a step toward me, fingers sliding under my jaw to lift my face. "More than anything in memory, yes. But I'm not sure how I feel about you being drunk."

"I'm not drunk. I'm Scottish."

He throws his head back and laughs. Before I can form a coherent response, he sobers, lips still curved as his gaze locks on my face. Then even the smile fades, and all I'm left with is the emotion burning in his eyes. It's a little scary, and so, so sexy.

The next thing I know, his arms are around my waist, yanking me onto my tiptoes. His hot, soft lips find mine, the scruff on his jaw teasing my chin and cheeks. I moan in gratitude and relief, wrapping my arms tightly around his shoulders. We feed from each other like every touch of our tongues is the first and last.

I soak in his heat and taste, my body burning, all pain gone. Disjointed thoughts tumble in my mind. *Yes. I need this. Him.* When I grab his hair, he groans. Hands slide from my waist to cup my ass, pulling me roughly against him. He's already hard, a thick line of heat against my stomach.

"We need to go now," he whispers breathlessly, "because I'm seriously considering tearing off your pants and taking you against that tree."

"Whatever you want," I say mindlessly. Then my remaining brain cells activate. I jerk back to stare at him. "What? Hell no."

He laughs, thrusting lightly to tease me. "You're too much. Come on."

Setting me down, he opens the passenger door of a sleek BMW. I sink into the heated leather seat with a sigh of bliss.

Beckett slides behind the wheel, sending me a searing look. "Buckle up."

I do, and as he pulls away from the curb, I impulsively grab his right hand and draw it into my lap. Bewitched by his nearness, driven by a confidence I've never before possessed, I lift my hips and guide him between my open legs. His jaw clenches, fingers curling possessively.

"I can feel your heat," he hisses, gaze slashing to me. "God, Iris, I need to be inside you."

"Eyes on the road," I murmur. My fingers atop his, I rock lightly against the heel of his hand.

"Bloody hell," he gasps.

My body completely given over to sensation, I let go

of my final inhibitions. Head falling back, eyes closing, I relish every rising swell of pleasure.

Our perfect rhythm never falters, and when he whispers, "That's it, ah fuck, Iris, you're so beautiful," dense, sparkling energy coalesces at the base of my spine.

"Don't stop. James... Oh—"

I climax with a shudder, catching my cry with my hands.

The car jerks to a stop and I open my eyes. We're parked in the driveway of a beautiful two-story home, white with dark trim, set behind a small, lush front yard.

I have no recollection of the journey. "Where are we?"

"Wallingford." He tears off his seatbelt and races around the car to my door. Wrenching it open, he growls, "Out, now."

Giggling, I unbuckle my seatbelt and take his hand, then yelp as he yanks me off my feet into his arms. Our faces close, I read the soft wonder in his eyes.

"Tell me that just happened."

I nip lightly at his lower lip. "Yes, I got off on your hand with all my clothes on. You're just that good."

He chuckles and kisses me hard. "Oh, pet, I haven't even begun."

A door slams somewhere close and a woman yells, "Who the fuck is that, James?"

The arms around me slacken. Without their support, I stumble back, my hip connecting with the open car door. I feel the pain only distantly, my mind and body suddenly, frigidly cold. At the top of the stairs leading to the picturesque porch and front door, a tall woman stands highlighted by the house lights.

"What the hell are you doing here?" asks Beckett in a tone I've never heard him use before. One as cold as I feel.

"Who is that?" I hear my voice ask.

He doesn't answer, but the woman does.

"I'm his wife."

9. ballad

James—no, *Beckett*—drives me home. Every time he opens his mouth, I tell him to shut up. Eventually he quits trying to explain, hopefully realizing there's not a damned thing he can say to make this better. He's married. The end.

When he stops outside my apartment building, I'm out of the car in seconds, running to the front door.

"Iris, *please!*" he yells through the open window.

The only sound I want to make is a scream. Clamping my lips shut, I tear open the door and dart across the lobby. I jab the elevator button repeatedly. It finally opens, and I crash into the person walking out.

The man grabs my shoulders to steady me. "Iris! What's wrong?"

I look up numbly at Griffen. "Nothing," I mumble, unable to meet his eyes.

"Not nothing," he says firmly. "You're crying. Did someone do something to you? Talk to me."

I glance involuntarily toward the front doors, but the BMW is gone. Relief and the beginnings of sanity flow into my brain.

"Sorry," I say, wiping my face quickly. "Really, I'm fine. Just get emotional when I drink."

I can tell he's unconvinced, but he doesn't press me. "If there's anything I can do to help, will you please tell me?"

"Yes, thanks," I say, ducking past him into the elevator.

The doors slowly close on his concerned face. His chivalry reminds me so much of my brother that by the time I reach the fifth floor, I'm sobbing. Horrible, half-drunk heaves that won't stop no matter how hard I try to hold them in.

The doors open on Claire, phone in hand. "God, Iris! Griff just texted me. Honey, come here." She pulls me from the wall and into the hallway, wrapping her arms tightly around me. "Tell me what happened. Who do I have to kill?"

I snort-sob into her shoulder. "I wish it was that

simple," I whisper, lifting my teary face to see hers. "He's married, Claire. Google didn't say he was married."

Her eyes widen. "Beckett? *That's* who picked you up? Jesus, this requires a drink."

She pulls me by the hand into our apartment and deposits me on the sofa. A minute later, she hands me a tumbler with a splash of whiskey. I swallow it, coughing at the burn on my raw throat.

Claire settles beside me. "Spill."

"I was going to do it. Sleep with him. I want... wanted him so much. More than... it's not rational, feeling this way." I take a shuddering breath. "He kissed me Wednesday night. In the rain. It was magic. Now it's a bad TV drama."

She pauses, absorbing the words. "How did you find out he's married?"

I laugh darkly. "She was at his house waiting for him. He'd just... we just..." I knuckle my eyes. "He'd just gotten me off on the car ride there. Clothes on. Just his hand outside my pants."

Claire sucks in a breath. "Uhh, wow. And his so-called wife? What was she doing?"

"Standing on the front porch. The light was behind her, so I couldn't see her very well... but she definitely saw us. She wasn't happy. Neither was he."

Claire rubs her forehead. "This is messed up. They

must be separated, right? I mean, he hasn't been exactly celibate since the quarter started."

I groan. "Has everyone but me seen him with a trail of well-used women behind him?"

"I've just heard rumors. But realistically, it was probably one woman not five. That's the nature of the telephone game. And the way he looks... he's like walking sex, all brooding and graceful and brilliant."

"Stop, please," I whisper.

Claire gasps in horror. "Fuck, Iris, I'm so sorry. I think I'm still kind of drunk."

"It's okay." I stand on unsteady legs. "I'm going to take a shower and pass out."

She rises to give me a tight hug. "Aww, honey. I wish there was something I do."

I shake my head mutely and head to my room. Collapsing on my bed, I suddenly want nothing more than to sleep. But fanciful or not, I can still smell him. Taste him.

With a groan of dismay, I roll off the bed and tear off my coat. My cell phone flies, landing on the comforter before me. Lifting it with a shaking hand, I press the home button until the screen lights up. Dreading... hoping...

Nothing.

I throw it down and head for the shower.

Sunday's storm passes before dawn, and Monday morning is one of those achingly clear fall days. Glistening asphalt and wet leaves. Air so cold it feels thick in your lungs. As I walk onto campus, I take it all in, acutely aware that this is the last October I'll spend here. Every step feels both new and like one I've taken a thousand times.

Four years of undergrad, two years of working and saving money to offset student loans, and two years of graduate school.

Eight down, one to go.

Almost there, Derrick.

Emboldened by the knowledge that I'm close to fulfilling the promise I made to my brother, I walk with renewed purpose into the English Department and up the stairs. Down the familiar hallway. Into the classroom already half-full of students. Beckett is at his desk, a dark presence to my left. I don't look at him as I move to my spot in the back.

As I sit, Janice turns around from a few rows up. "Iris, you chopped off your hair!"

I shrug, fingering the shoulder-length strands. "It was time."

"It's so pretty and wavy," she says warmly, "and you look so much older."

I smile faintly. "That's what I keep hearing," I reply, and pull out my laptop.

The remaining students filter in over the next minutes. There are several more flattering comments about my hair, which make me both glad of the impulsive visit to the salon yesterday and increasingly self-conscious.

Beckett, I notice, doesn't lift his head from his notebook once.

At nine o'clock, he stands and begins the lecture. I might be imagining it, but his voice seems less vibrant than usual. I tell myself I don't care.

I don't care.

But when I finally raise my eyes to his face and see how tired he looks, melancholy descends on my shoulders.

I do care. Too much.

The urge to wipe away his frown and make him smile is an itch that intensifies over the next hour. To combat it, I pull up Google on my laptop and search with keywords *James S. Beckett* and *wife*.

There's one picture of them together, dated two years ago at a gala hosted by the Academy of American Poets. A former winner of the Lenore Marshall Poetry Prize for the book of poems he published while at Stanford, Beckett had been in attendance to present the same award.

The photo is familiar, as this weekend I spent a fair amount of time staring at it—more than was healthy, to be sure. But it helps to be reminded now. To see the wicked smile on his face. The way his fingers curl around her hip. Her name is Julia. She's gorgeous, with auburn hair and classic beauty à la Bette Davis. The cameraman caught her looking up at him in adoration.

I know there's a narrative I can't see in the two-dimensional image. The story of them, written beneath the ice that coated his voice. The rage and desperation in her statement, *I'm his wife*. But in my searching, nowhere did I find mention of a divorce.

I almost slept with a married man.

"Ms. Eliot, if you'll join us?"

His sharp voice jerks me in my seat. I quickly close my laptop and meet his vivid eyes.

"Sorry," I fumble, "I was reviewing—"

"Thank you," he interjects. "While you were daydreaming, we were discussing the short stories due next week and the process of workshopping them. As you'll be facilitating, it might be wise to pay attention."

The room is deathly quiet. Flushing angrily, I bite

back the instinct to snap at him. "Absolutely, professor. My apologies again."

He glares at me for another moment, then returns his attention to what's less of a discussion and more of a list of commands.

Terrance, sitting adjacent to me, whispers, "Asshole." I shoot him a tight smile and start taking notes.

Twenty minutes later, we're dismissed with a curt, "That's all."

I pack up and squeeze out the door between two students, sighing in relief once I'm in the hallway. Terrance catches up to me near the elevator.

"Iris, do you know what Beckett's deal is? He was a dick all class. Are we really doing that badly?"

"No," I assure him. "I'm sure it's, uh, personal stuff or something. Keep writing, Terrance. I really like where you're headed so far."

He smiles broadly. "Thanks! See you tomorrow."

I nod and take the elevator downstairs, then head into the hallway hosting faculty offices. Even though coffee sounds wonderful, I avoid the busy lounge, not willing to risk running into Beckett.

Thankfully, the small office I share with two other TAs is empty. I close the door and sink listlessly onto the chair behind the desk. After several numb minutes of staring at the wall, I pull myself together and open my laptop. The picture of Beckett and his wife is still open. I quickly close the window and bring up my current assignment due Wednesday evening.

Beckett wants an original short story with a minimum of eight thousand words.

So far, I have a total of six.

Everything changed on a rainy night.

"Crap," I hiss, deleting the words.

The door opens. I look up, expecting a TA. The smile I've just begun mustering freezes and cracks.

"Go away," I tell Beckett.

He cocks a brow and steps inside, closing the door soundly. Leaning a hip on the other side of the desk, he crosses his arms and stares down at me.

I armor myself with memory of that picture, and repeat coldly, "Go. Away."

He sighs, glancing out the window above my head. "Whether you want to or not, you're going to let me explain," he says crisply. "Julia and I have been separated for more than a year. We were barely married eight months before we split. She won't sign the papers until I grant her custody, which I will never fucking do."

I rock back in shock. "You have a *child* with her?"

His gaze snaps down, expression slack with horror. "God, no." He shakes his head, scrubbing fingers through his hair. "Sorry. Stuck my foot in my mouth, there. Not a child. A dog. He's *my* bloody dog."

I release a deranged laugh. "Great, okay. Good luck with everything. Now, will you go away?"

"Iris," he murmurs urgently, "please, don't turn your back on this. On us."

"There is no us!" I snap, then wince at the volume of my voice. "We've kissed twice. And had that... whatever in the car. It's nothing."

"It wasn't nothing," he retorts.

I'm on a roll, though, and barely pause. "This whole situation is stopping right now. It's taking up way too much space in my head—space I need to, you know, *graduate*. You really want to know what makes me tick?" I spread my arms. "This. Finishing my masters is the single most important thing in my life, and I will not allow my stupid heart to derail everything I've worked so hard for!"

The words vibrate, echoing between my ears. When I realize what I've said, the blood drains from my face.

Beckett stills, eyes bright and unblinking. "Your heart?" he whispers. "Iris—"

I rocket to my feet, swipe my laptop off the desk, and rush toward the door. I'm reaching for the handle when he grabs my arm, spinning me toward him. My laptop is snatched from my fingers and tossed onto the tiny couch.

Gentle fingers move through my hair, exploring the shorter strands. His forearms blind my peripherals, creating a soft, dark space where only he and I exist. I can hear my breath, shallow and fast. My fingers clench at his waist.

I whisper his name.

Hands frame my face, lifting it. "God help us both," he whispers.

And his mouth takes possession of mine.

10. blank verse

The world shifts on its axis. Or maybe I'm not getting enough oxygen. But in this moment, I don't care. Our kiss quickly escalates to sucking, biting madness. His hands claim my breasts, fingers finding my nipples, tugging hard enough to send liquid lightning to my core. I palm him roughly through his pants. He grunts, his hips jerking forward.

I remember his typed words—*we're both nervous I'm too big for you*—but feeling him thick and heavy behind his zipper, I'm not nervous at all. I'm electrified.

"I need you," he whispers against my mouth.

This is insanity.

Someone could walk in any second.

"Yes," I gasp.

His belt buckle yields to my scrambling fingers. I

manage to pull pants and boxers to his thighs before I'm lifted. Braced in one arm, his other hand goes to work yanking down my jeans. Somehow, I kick off my boots, all the while feasting on the smooth, delicious skin of his neck. He hoists me up with forearms beneath my thighs. I wrap my legs eagerly around him, whimpering as one finger, then two, sink into me.

He muffles a groan in my hair, then twists, searching for something on the desk. There's a muted tearing, and his hand angles between us. *Condom,* I think distantly. He adjusts me in his arms, backing me against the wall beside the door. The sound of footsteps and voices through the barrier is terrifying. And makes me even hotter. Wetter.

"Please," I whisper.

He teases my entrance with the head of his cock, sliding it back and forth, back and forth, until my fingers dig deep into his shoulders. I whimper, and he finally enters me, one slow inch at a time, until he's fully seated and pressing against my absolute limit.

I've never felt so consumed, so full of another person. Taking a fold of his sweater between my teeth, I bite down hard against the urge to cry out.

His low voice warms my ear. "I'm seriously five seconds away. This is ridiculous. You feel too perfect."

My hips rock, obeying a biological command. He

sucks in a breath, arms flexing to assist my movement, guiding me harder and faster. Fullness and friction build to a blinding peak, dissembling every last shred of intellect.

I am simple. I am animal.

His teeth nip my earlobe. "So sweet. Iris, you undo me. God, you're close. I can feel it. Take it, love."

I do, bucking against him, a whimper in my throat as I come undone. Seconds later, he makes a strangled sound and stills, pulsing heavily inside me.

Our mouths meet unerringly. The kiss is drowning deep, a swallowing of souls. My womb pulses with an aftershock; he twitches inside me, still half-hard.

Slowly, the ringing in my ears subsides. In the office next to ours, voices laugh. A door opens and closes down the hall. In fits and starts, my brain comes back online.

"Oh my God," I breathe, leaning back to see his face.

His eyes are a soft, verdant shade as he brushes a strand of hair from my cheek. "I was thinking a bed for our first time, but that will do."

Gasping back laughter, I wiggle in his arms. "Put me down. We have to get dressed."

With a final kiss and soft chuckle, he does. As he takes care of the condom, I swiftly pull on my underwear and jeans, then sit on the couch to tie my boots. When I look up, his slacks are on, though still unbuttoned.

"I have no idea how we go about this," he says, smiling slightly. "Should I pull the fire alarm, perhaps?"

My gaze falls to the floor as I recall Kirk's story about witnessing the aftermath of this exact situation. A woman looking the worse for wear as she slipped from Beckett's office.

My afterglow fades under a tide of uneasiness. *He's done this before.*

"Iris?" he asks carefully.

I force a laugh and look up. "Don't be silly. We'll wait until the hallway is clear. You leave first. I need to work on Wednesday's assignment, anyway, and I have class in an hour. I'll, uh... open the window for a bit."

His gaze sharpens, but at length he nods. I watch him button his pants, fasten his belt, and step into his fine Italian loafers. After adjusting his shirt and sweater, he drags fingers through his hair. My lips quirk, as the action only messes it further.

Walking to the door, he leans an ear briefly against it, then turns to fix a penetrating stare on my face. "I'll be honest, I'm a little unnerved by your lack of visible emotion right now. Am I the only one who just had mind-blowing sex in an unlocked office?"

I flush, shaking my head. "No. That was great. Thanks."

Beckett's brows skyrocket, his head shaking in bafflement. Unable to hold his gaze, I look down, picking imaginary lint off my thighs. He makes a harsh noise, somewhere between caustic laughter and a grunt.

"Well, then. At least I know where we stand."

The cutting tone shivers against the broken place inside me. Leaning back in the couch, I stare flatly at him.

"I'm a student, you're a professor. Familiar ground for you, isn't it? If we're found out, at most you'll get a slap on the wrist, but I'll be shunned by the entire department. Not only that, you're married—separated or not—and you said it yourself, you don't date." I pause, tilting my head. "What exactly do you want from me, Beckett? Do you want me to drop out and be your modern-day concubine?"

He flinches in shock, then anger pinches his lips. "That's rich. Very mature of you, to lash out when you're emotionally compromised."

The brokenness inside me expands, swallowing me whole. I make a show of looking around. "I'm sorry, am I in the wrong room? The only emotions I have where you're concerned are lust and anger. And now, regret."

As soon as the words leave my lips, I want to take them back. I watch miserably as his expression blanks, his cheeks paling noticeably.

I've hurt him. Badly.

I gasp, "James, I—"

"Don't bother," he snaps, his accent suddenly thick. "Now that the devil has revealed herself, I find myself immune to her angelic pretenses. It's a fucking miracle I didn't do something stupid like invite you into my actual bed."

Without bothering to check for passersby, he throws open the door and leaves.

Moments later, I hear a female voice ask, "Beckett, are you all right?"

"Stupendous, Francine," he says, with intentional clarity so his words reach my ears. "What are you doing for dinner tonight?"

———————————————

When I arrive home after my poetry class, I find Claire and Griffen on the couch. The television is on, but from their flushed faces I've clearly interrupted more than a Doctor Who marathon. Their well-meaning offer to relocate to Claire's bedroom abruptly changes my plans. No way can I get any work done with them getting frisky on the other side of my wall.

"I'm just going to take a shower and head to the library." Before they can protest, I add, "Really, don't worry about it. I have a short story and three haikus to write, anyway."

In my bathroom, I turn on the shower as hot as it will go and quickly disrobe. I don't look in the mirror. I can't handle facing the scars right now—but even more so, I don't want to see evidence of sex with Beckett. From the ache in my thighs, where I'm sure there are red imprints from his fingers, to the warmth on my neck where his teeth sank deeply.

Stepping beneath the scalding flow, I let the heat melt away the knots in my shoulders, the lingering stiffness in my back and legs. There's nothing to be done about the soreness between my legs.

Every time I move, I feel the echo of him inside me. It's torture and pleasure; as much as I can't stand it, I thrill in it.

And I wish, more than anything, that I wasn't broken. That I was bold and brave, and capable of admitting, *Yes, I'm emotionally compromised. It's crazy because I've known you less than three weeks, but I have feelings for you. I want to know everything about you. I want to be yours.*

If I'm honest, it happened the first moment I saw him. Before he ever looked up from his journal. Something in my heart quickened when I saw him writing, a conduit for his raging muse. His ink-stained left hand.

When I see you, something... changes in me.

He feels it, too. The singing promise of something big. Poetic and beautiful.

A potential for real love.

Not the kind of love that takes advantage of an innocent sixteen-year-old girl. That invites her to a party, drugs her, and nearly rapes her. Not the kind that compels that young girl's brother—home from college for spring break—to track her phone when she doesn't answer his calls.

My brother found me before... *before.* Derrick beat that boy I thought I loved bloody, then threw him out of the bedroom. He dressed my limp body and carried me to his car.

I remember him yelling at me, demanding, *"What the fuck were you thinking?"* and, *"Iris, wake up! I need you to open your eyes!"*

I found out later that he was driving me to the hospital. Despite his fear for my wellbeing, he was going the speed limit. Sober as a judge. We would have made it if the drunk driver hadn't caught us in the middle of an intersection.

I don't remember the event, but I've read the police report. The other driver was going fifty-eight miles per hour. Derrick's small pickup hadn't stood a chance. We flipped three times and smashed into a telephone pole.

The gas tank ruptured. Live wires fell, sparking, on top of us.

Good Samaritans pulled my unconscious body from the burning car. I was covered in blood from twenty-eight lacerations of varying degrees on my torso, arms, and legs. Shattered knee, broken shoulder. Second degree burns along my left side from armpit to thigh.

The only parts of me uninjured were my face, neck, and upper chest. A miracle, according to family and friends. A statistical anomaly, according to the doctors who treated me.

But I know the truth. It was Derrick, flinging himself as best he could atop me in those final moments. Using his last breaths to shield me from the fire and exploding glass.

To protect me, just like always.

11. cacophony

I don't end up at the library; I can't be on campus right now. Where he is. Instead, I put on sneakers and my knee brace for added support and walk outside. Clouds boil overhead in warning, but the rain isn't supposed to start until tonight.

So I walk, my muscles slowly warming, my damp hair tucked under a beanie and hood. I don't stop for several miles, and then only because my phone vibrates in my pocket.

Pulling it out, I read the Caller ID and quickly answer. During the school term, my mother and I rarely speak outside our Sunday morning calls.

"Mom? What's wrong?"

She's quiet for a few moments; my stomach drops. "I

don't know how to say this, baby. So I'm just going to tell you. Your father died today."

The first, strongest emotion is apathy.

"Okay."

Another pause. "Would you like to know what happened?"

"He had a heart attack while banging a twenty-year-old?" I ask sharply, then blanch. "Jesus, mom. I'm sorry."

She sighs. "No, it's all right. It *was* a heart attack, actually. During a seminar on campus."

Nebulous thoughts bounce through me, oddly linked. Stanford campus, where he's been a professor for thirty years.

Never slept with his students, at least.

Beckett sleeps with students.

Dad preferred waitresses, I recall.

Why did I never see the connection?

Charming philanderers.

Is this the Freudian Electra complex?

Yuck, yuck. Quadruple Yuck.

"Iris?" asks my mom.

"I'm here," I say, then clear my throat. "Are you going to the memorial? I'm assuming there will be one."

"Yes, I think so."

My father did love my mother—deeply. Anyone who's read his poetry knows that. But love wasn't enough for him to keep it in his pants. Haunted by the unnamed need to find his next great inspiration, he turned his back on her and on his children.

He never did find another muse.

Mom finally left him when Derrick and I were old enough to understand. We unanimously agreed with the divorce. In the final years, he was rarely home anyway, opting to live in an apartment near campus.

"Would you like to fly down and come with me?" she asks.

I take a breath. "Let me think about it, okay? My workload is pretty intense this quarter."

It's a weak excuse, but beneath my shell of apathy stirs old resentment. Why should I show up for his funeral when he couldn't show up for even one of my dance recitals?

"Of course, baby. When I get the details, I'll email them to you."

"Thanks, mom." I hesitate. "I'm sorry."

She makes a small sound. "Me, too. I wish he'd lived a happier life."

"Yeah," I say vaguely.

"I love you, Iris."

"Love you, too, mom. Bye."

I tuck my phone back in my pocket and stare at the sky, now darkening to ominous pewter. Turning stiffly, I begin the long walk home. The brace on my knee is a lifesaver on the steady uphill grade, but I'm still in pain by the time I reach my building. It's raining lightly now, and the ground is slick.

My head down to make sure I take the steps of my building carefully, I almost fall over the man sitting at the top. Strong hands catch me as I wobble.

"This is becoming a habit," Beckett says softly.

My heart trips down to my knees. "What are you doing here?" I demand, looking around. "This is a mostly student building. You shouldn't be here."

Belatedly, I realize his expression is one of profound sympathy. And before he speaks, I know why he's come.

"I heard about your father." He stands, rain misting around his uncovered head and dusting the shoulders of his coat.

My brows lift. "So you decided to sit outside my building on the off chance I came outside?"

"I was working up the nerve to call you." He pauses. "I'm so sorry for your loss, Iris."

I shrug. "Don't be. I haven't spoken with him since Derrick's funeral. He brought a date who happened to be fifteen years younger than him." The uncertainty on Beckett's face brings acidic words to my lips. "Oh, I'm sorry. He probably taught you at Stanford. Did you worship him like everyone else?"

His lips thin. "Stop, Iris. For the love of God, stop pushing me away."

I glance behind him. "Where's Francine? Aren't you supposed to be having dinner?"

My callous words have an effect opposite of the one I'd anticipated. He laughs, a light, bright sound that spreads cracks through my shell of indifference. Before I can make sense of his reaction, his warm hand cups my cold cheek. A thumb brushes my temple.

"I'm sorry I said that," he murmurs, smile softening. "I reacted out of anger and hurt. It took me a while to sort through why you said those awful things."

"Because I meant them?"

He shakes his head. "You're afraid of what's happening between us."

"There is no us," I say, but faintly.

His eyes darken, fastening on my lips. "Tell me what I have to do for you to give me a chance."

A whirlwind of hope, fear, lust, and dread cycles through me. I step back until his hand falls, needing distance.

Needing... I don't fucking know.

I tell him, "I can't do this right now. I have so much work—I haven't even started my short story."

"I'll give you an extension."

"I don't want special treatment!" I snap.

"Your father just died," he says gently. "It's not special treatment."

Two students walk past us up the stairs. Hearing Beckett's words, they cast me concerned glances. "I'm fine," I say with a tight smile. "Everything's fine. Move along."

Concern turns to annoyance, and they disappear inside.

Beckett snorts. "Ah, Iris. You're in a class of your own."

I pinch the bridge of my nose, squinting at him over my fingers. "What do you want from me? Seriously, tell me. I'm totally overwhelmed right now."

His eyes soften at my raw tone. "To be close to you. And so much more. But right now, all I really want is for you to tell me today wasn't a mistake. That you don't regret it."

Darkness shivers inside me, but it's not the broken place this time. It's a sweet, sensual awakening, a languorous stretch of feminine power.

"I went for a walk so I could feel you in every step. Does that answer your question?"

He stills, lower lip falling. A flush blooms high on his cheekbones. In a broken whisper, he asks, "Where on Earth did you come from?"

Pleased beyond reasonable levels by his reaction, I

smirk. "San Francisco."

"Thank you, San Francisco," he breathes, then takes a step closer to me. Several more students walk past us, and he freezes. "Damnit."

I sigh. "That's not going to change. You know that, right? Not for another year."

He nods, staring into the distance. "I do." Gaze meeting mine, he adds softly, "I'm at a loss."

See me in secret. We'll be careful.

But aloud I say, "Maybe by next year, you'll be divorced. And have different feelings about dating."

I don't mean for the words to be so solemn and firm. But I don't take them back, because they're true. I don't want shame and secrecy. Not even if it means I can have him.

Beckett laughs softly, but the sadness of it squeezes my heart. "Straight to the point as usual, pet. Message received. And for what it's worth, I'm proud of you." He hesitates, expression smoothing to professional distance. "Please let me know if you need an extension on the assignment. I'll take over the workshop tomorrow morning." As I start to protest, he shakes his head. "I'm your boss, remember?"

I nod, and he turns, walking lightly down the steps.

No... Wait!

I stand frozen until he's gone.

Over the next several weeks, I pour all of my focus into school. Study. Write. Grade. Teach. Write. Every spare minute I have, I fill with networking potential job opportunities for next year, meeting with the two other faculty members on my Thesis Committee, and generally avoiding Beckett like the plague.

It's not easy, as I have to see him at minimum twice weekly. But so far, we've maintained emotional and physical distance. He doesn't tease me, touch me, or push my buttons anymore. For my part, I avoid eye contact as much as possible and stay at least five feet away from him at all times. No tempting heat or mouthwatering scent to override my survival methods.

Late evening is the only time I really struggle. Those hours when I'm not tired enough to sleep but too braindead to enjoy any form of social life. Not calling, texting, or emailing Beckett is a daily battle. Finally, when I can't take it anymore, I fish out an unused box of stationary from my closet.

I write him letters. Never to be sent or read, but I don't need a psychology degree to know they're not really for him. Pouring out my thoughts is cathartic. The best kind of therapy.

I hold nothing back, detailing events and thoughts

from childhood all the way to the present day. My promise to Derrick. His obsession with hockey and my sweatshirt talisman. His inexplicable love of sauerkraut. The night of the accident, my injuries and my rehabilitation. The first time a boyfriend in college saw my scars and made excuses to leave, then never called me again. My stepsisters, who are both great, loving people, but who I'm afraid to care about.

The new novel I've started drafting. My favorite of his books, my favorite poem from his published collection. My favorite poem of my father's, about the night he met my mother. My favorite songs, foods, and movies. My passion for dance, that still lives in me despite my knee injury. My obsession with historical romance novels. My undying love for early British punk music.

On and on and on.

In tens of letters I'll never send, I tell him everything that makes me tick.

12. canto

The afternoon of Halloween, Claire storms into the living room and delivers an ultimatum: "Either you dress up and come out with me or I'm firing you as my best friend."

Curled into a corner of the couch with a cup of tea and a book, I don't bother looking up. "I'm not putting on a slutty witch costume and getting drunk in public. Halloween is the stupidest adult holiday ever."

She gasps in exaggerated horror. "You did *not* just say that!"

I roll my eyes and take a sip of my tea. "Besides, three's a crowd. I'm not interested in chatting up random dudes while you and Griffen make out in a corner."

She snatches the book out of my hands and throws it down on the coffee table.

"What the hell, Claire!"

"Exactly!" she snaps, pointing a finger at me. "What the hell! You've been a zombie for three weeks. You won't talk about Beckett or your dad, and every time I invite you out, you tell me you have to study. You've lost weight, you're not sleeping, and if I have to listen to one more record by The Damned, I'm going to burn the house down!"

I blink, unsure whether to laugh or cry at her tirade. I settle on, "I didn't know you felt that way."

Sighing gustily, she sinks onto the couch. "Please, please come out tonight. It's our last college Halloween. We're not going to a stupid house party, anyway."

I immediately start shaking my head. "No way—"

"Yes," she cuts me off, "we're going to the faculty party. But don't worry, Beckett won't be there. Griffen made sure to ask him after class on Wednesday. He said something along the lines of, 'not a chance in hell.' Pretty sure that means you're in the clear."

I groan. "You guys conspired against me."

She nods, unaffected. "We care about you. I hate seeing you this way, and I miss my best friend. Come. Please."

"Last college Halloween," I murmur.

She grins, triumphant. "Yes. And I won't make you wear my slutty witch costume."

"But I don't have—"

"Yes, you do."

She flies off the couch and grabs a garment bag from the hall closet. Unzipping it with a flourish, she displays the costume inside.

I look at it for a long moment, then swing my incredulously gaze to her. "Seriously? A fairy? Why do you hate me?"

Claire just laughs. "Not just any fairy," she says proudly. "The Fairy Queen."

The cosmetic gold glitter Claire applied across my eyelids and temples is starting to mess with my vision, giving sparkling haloes to bodies and inanimate objects alike. Or it might be the compounding effects of the green punch—suspiciously strong for a faculty gathering. I'd almost refused it, but Claire had stood with me for ten minutes while I watched people ladling and drinking with no ill effects.

Once my anxiety subsided, she commandeered the entire punch bowl, not allowing anyone near as she poured our drinks. For herself, she went the standard single-cup route, but for me, she filled a thermos so I wouldn't have to face the bowl again.

Now, feeling warm and loose from the punch and dreamy from my glittery vision, I tell her, "You're the greatest wing-woman in the world, Claire-bear."

She giggles, looking up at me from her cozy seat beside Griffen. They're dressed as Odysseus and Penelope of Homer's *Odyssey*. Anywhere else, they'd be pegged as nothing more specific than Greek gods. But this is, after all, a party of academics.

I've already had four different people quote Shakespeare's *A Midsummer Night's Dream* to me.

"Did you see Dr. Alcott?" whispers Griffen, making an unsubtle gesture of his head.

I nod, biting my lips against laughter as I look across the room. Dr. Alcott is the Head of the Philosophy Department and also hosting the party at his home. He's dressed in an extravagant owl costume—representing the companion of Minerva, Roman goddess of wisdom. I'll admit, I was stumped when I saw him. Until someone explained it to me, I thought he was a sports-team mascot.

Presently, his narrow, flushed face is visible, the headpiece lifted as he speaks with a man dressed in all black who could be anything from Dracula to a space singularity. And though I can't see the man's face, his presence tickles my senses. There's something familiar about his short blond hair, and how he's standing... I blink hard and the world momentarily morphs into a disco ball.

"Who are you staring at?" asks Claire excitedly, leaning forward to follow my gaze. She immediately gasps. "Holy shit, is that Brad?"

Griffen leans forward. "Brad Fowler? Oh yeah, it's definitely him." He glances at Claire. "Should I be worried that you look so thrilled?"

She elbows him, jerking her head toward me. I start to roll my eyes, but decide against it as the room shifts a little.

Claire grins evilly at me. "Iris, go say hi."

"Nope. No."

"Weren't you two good friends?" asks Griffen in confusion. I nod hesitantly, and before I can stop him, he shouts, "Fowler! Over here!"

Brad glances in our direction. When he sees Griffen, he waves and excuses himself from Alcott. As he walks toward us, I try to melt into the space between a side table and the wall and even consider ducking behind a nearby plant.

Halfway across the room, Brad's gaze lands on me. A huge smile lights his face. I'm so stunned that he isn't running in the opposite direction, all I can do is stare as he walks quickly to me and pulls me into a hug.

"Iris, it's so good to see you," he says happily. "How are you?"

"Good," I squeak.

Taking me by the shoulders, his gaze flows to my feet and back. "You look amazing. Either Titania or maybe one of the Celtic goddesses. Cerridwen? Brigid?"

I shrug. "Just a woodland fairy."

He laughs, glancing at Claire. "You made her come, didn't you?" She winks.

Brad slides his arm around my shoulders, tucking me into his side in a way that's so familiar it's like putting on my favorite pajamas. Looking down at me, he says, "You're probably the only person in the room who can guess who I am tonight."

I take in the white dress shirt under the black coat, perfectly creased ascot, and finally, the tiny spectacles in his breast pocket.

Laughing, I say, "W.B. Yeats."

His smile softens. "Nothing's changed," he says, then gives me a quick, hot kiss on my forehead. As I'm reeling from the contact, I happen to look across the room toward the front door.

A man stands in the entryway staring at me. Green eyes fix on Brad's arm around my shoulders, then flicker to my forehead where I was just kissed. And finally, he looks into my eyes.

Pain.

Longing.

Anger.

Resignation.

Defeat.

Brad is wrong—*everything* has changed.

"Excuse me," I gasp as I bolt after Beckett.

Behind me, Claire calls, "Iris? Where are you going?"

"Bathroom!" I blurt.

When I reach the entryway, Beckett is gone. *Where is he?* I spin wildly but can't see him anywhere. With just enough wits left not to yell his name, I open the front door and run down the walkway. It's freezing and late, the moon a sinister sliver in the black sky. The sidewalks in both directions are empty.

No!

Out of habit, I reach for my phone in my pocket, but I'm wearing what amounts to tights and a fucking tutu. My small purse is inside with Claire.

Teeth chattering, I whisper, "Goddamnit, James, where did you go?"

"You ran right past me, pet."

With a strangled gasp, I whirl back toward the house. He's sitting alone on a white porch swing, elbows braced on his knees. There's limited light, but I can feel the weight of gaze on me.

I stand frozen, having not thought this far ahead.

Softly, he murmurs, "'*Yes, fancy, come, my fairy love, these throbbing temples softly kiss; and bend my lonely couch above, and bring me rest, and bring me bliss.*'"

I'm not certain, but I think it's Emily Brontë. When I don't move, or say anything, he sighs.

"Go back inside, Iris. It's glacial out here."

The dam inside me breaks. I have to tell him. *Tell him.* "Brad's just a friend. He lives in Oregon. I haven't seen him since he graduated in spring."

After a long pause, he says mildly, "You're pissed."

"No... what? I'm not mad. I just didn't want you to think... or, um, misunderstand."

His smile gleams in the shadows. "Pissed as in drunk. Plastered. Sloshed."

"Ohh," I say, nodding. "British drunk."

His low chuckle is music to my ears. My body finally back in my command, I walk toward him, wrapping arms around my torso to conserve body heat. I make it to the edge of the porch and stop. Even sloshed and aching for him, I remember my five-feet rule.

"Griffen said you weren't coming."

He shrugs. "I wasn't. Then the last trick-or-treater

came and went, and it was just me and a bowl of snickers. Rufus didn't even want to play."

I snort. "Your dog's name is Rufus?"

His brows lift in affront. "It's a perfectly respectable name."

I cough over laughter. "Yes, definitely. It's a great name."

Beckett shifts forward, hands clenching on his knees. He whispers fiercely, "You're standing there shivering, and all I want in the world is to wrap you in blankets and serve you tea. And I can't even offer you my coat, because any second someone is going to walk outside. So please, if you care at all for my honor, go inside where it's warm."

My heart thumps madly in my chest. "I don't want to," I say, possessed by the sweet darkness only he coaxes free. "Blankets and tea, huh?"

He makes a soft noise and jerks to his feet. "A thousand blankets. Any tea you want. I'll even let you defile it with sugar."

Adrenaline races through me, making me faintly dizzy. Searching his face, I say tremulously, "I'm not safe right now."

For some unknown reason, he knows exactly what I'm telling him—asking him.

"Even if you beg me to, I won't kiss you. Not tonight. You're safe with me, love."

Love.

Inexplicably, tears fill my eyes. "I'd really like blankets and tea. With you."

He steals toward me, fast and fluid. In seconds, he's whipped off his leather jacket and swung it around my shoulders. His scent and heat surround me. I sigh in relief.

Taking my fingers in his, he guides me down the walkway, across the sidewalk, and into the street. When we make it to the opposite sidewalk, he stops. I look up at him, registering his frown.

"What about the party?" he asks urgently. "This is crazy. Your purse, your friends..."

"I'll text Claire from your phone." When his brows jerk up, I smile. "Did you really think I wouldn't tell my best friend?"

He sighs through his teeth. "I suppose not. But people must have seen you leave—"

I shake my head roughly. "You're asking for a lot of concentration from an inebriated woman, Beckett. Let me think... Since no one came after me, I'm betting Claire saw you, saw me follow you, and is covering for me. So I'll text her with a cover story. I, uh, got my period and didn't want to wing it as Bloody Fairy, so I borrowed a phone to call my stepsister, who came and got me."

He barks a laugh. "God Almighty."

"Nope, just Aunt Flo," I quip, then slap my free hand to my mouth. Beckett's expression is a mix of hilarity and shock, and I can tell he's trying hard not laugh at me. "I'm not actually—that is... Ah, fuck. I'm drunk."

A grin teases his lips. "Since we're on the topic, it's forty degrees and I have no coat. My balls are the size of raisins, so I don't care what story you tell, just that we get in the car."

I screw up my face. "We're gross."

He laughs and tugs me into motion again. Luckily, his car's not far. Within seconds of starting the engine, heat flows over the popsicles that used to be my legs.

"Money *does* buy happiness," I proclaim, closing my eyes and stretching my feet toward the vents.

"No, it doesn't," he says, a smile in his voice, "but I'm hoping tea might."

That's a good bet.

I think I say it aloud, but I'm not sure. Not sure of anything, except that I'm warm and safe with James.

Wake me up when we're home.

"I will, love. Rest now."

13. catharsis

Sunlight flickers in my eyes, dancing through barren branches outside a large picture window. It's the first thing I notice, the glare being what woke me. The second thing I notice is luxuriously soft sheets on my bare arms and legs.

Bare arms and legs.

Springing upright, I clutch sheet and blankets to my body—still clothed, thank God, in the costume's corset top and skirt. The stays in back drape loosely but aren't completely undone. Mind racing, I peek under the covers to confirm the horrible truth.

Beneath wrinkled tulle, beautifully embroidered with beads and flowers, my tights are gone. I quickly drop the covers, then spy two strips of emerald silk at the foot of the bed. My gloves, that Claire had specially commissioned for my costume. Extra-long to hide the scars on my forearms and biceps.

My chest squeezes with panic. My eyes bounce erratically around, cataloging details of the bedroom. Dove grey walls, white molding, dark floorboards, rustic furniture. There's a cozy armchair by the window draped with a soft, butterscotch blanket. No pictures or knickknacks on the dresser. The closet door is open, but no clothes hang inside.

"Guest bedroom," I tell myself, voice shaking. "Relax. It was probably dark. He didn't see. Underwear intact. Nothing happened."

I drag cold fingers through my hair; they snag on the silk flowers stuck into several braids. The rest of what I feel is an unholy mess. With a sinking feeling, I remember the elaborate makeup and carefully touch my face. Surprisingly, my fingers come away with only minimal glitter.

I glance back at the pillow I slept on.

"Shit."

It's covered in gold.

A footstep creaks on a floorboard outside the room. I freeze and hold my breath, praying he didn't hear me talking to myself. *What the hell happened last night?* I don't remember anything past being in a warm car.

"Iris?" asks Beckett softly through the door. "Are you awake?"

"No!" I blurt.

He chuckles, and I hear a distinctly canine whine. "I'm going to leave some clothes outside the door. Bathroom is across the hall. And in case you're a little muddled, we texted Claire last night. She knows you're safe."

I sigh in relief. "Okay, thanks."

A floorboard creaks again. "I have aspirin for you when you come downstairs. And breakfast." He hesitates. "Do you need anything else right now?"

"Nope," I croak.

"Okay." A moment later, I hear his fading footsteps.

Flopping back onto the bed, I push the heels of my hands into my eyes. Disjointed memories emerge from the fog in my pounding head, each one more embarrassing than the last. A living room with a cozy fire. Me, stumbling around like a drunken idiot trying to pull off my tights. Babbling about letters and secrets and green punch.

Throwing my gloves at him. Throwing *myself* at him.

The rest is still fuzzy.

Eventually, humiliation fades enough for logic to make a reappearance. *Go downstairs. Pretend like nothing happened. Ask him to drive you home. Hide in your bed for at least twenty-four hours.*

Taking a breath for courage, I throw back the covers and walk across the room to open the door. Folded neatly on the ground are a long-sleeved thermal shirt and sweatpants, both of which I know I'll swim in. I pick them up, holding them to my face to breathe in faint detergent and an undercurrent of his scent. The temptation to wear them is too great; without further thought, I dart into the open bathroom and close the door.

On the counter beside the sink there's a new bar of soap and a washcloth. I set to work cleaning the circus-show of my smeared makeup and removing the flowers and braids from my hair. I'm able to work out the worst of the knots and finger comb the rest into some semblance of order.

The costume crumples to the floor, a mess of satin and tulle that hopefully a dry cleaner can salvage. Grateful for the last-minute decision to wear a bandeau under the corset, I pull on Beckett's shirt and shimmy into the sweatpants. I knot the waistband tightly and roll the sleeves to my wrists.

Saving me—barely—from looking like a teenager are the remnants of eyeliner and mascara and the cling of his shirt on my chest.

"Not too late to climb out a window," I offer my reflection.

Without shoes. Money. Or a phone.

"Right," I answer myself. "Breakfast it is."

Turning my back on vanity, I open the bathroom door. The mouthwatering scents of coffee and bacon tease my nose, luring me down the hallway to the stairs.

Descending slowly, I look around the large, modern space, decorated in a way that is quintessentially James Beckett. Masculine, elegant, minimalist.

The sight of the coffee table triggers a blurred memory of me standing on it. Shaking my head to banish the vision, I make my way to the threshold of the kitchen. And stop. And stare.

Beckett is feeding bacon to a small horse.

I must make a sound because both man and dog look at me. The next seconds happen in slow motion, at least in my world, which has abruptly narrowed to the avaricious gleam in the dog's eyes. Paws scramble on the ground, nails scratching over floor tiles. Beckett tries to grab the beast's collar. Misses.

"Rufus, no!"

The command perks dark ears, but it's too little too late. With a powerful bunching of hind legs, the German Shepherd launches himself at me. I cover my face with my hands and brace for impact, hoping there's nothing sharp or hard behind my head.

Forelegs descend heavily on my shoulders, but just... rest there. I peek hesitantly through my fingers, and a huge pink tongue swipes the revealed portion of my face. Then he's gone, dragged back by Beckett.

"Sit." Rufus obeys, tail wagging and tongue lolling as he grins up at me. "Iris, are you all right?" His tone is concerned, but his eyes sparkle with amusement.

"I'm good." With a small laugh, I take a step toward Rufus. "Can I, uh, pet him?"

Beckett grins. "Since he considers you his new best friend, I'm sure he'd love it."

I trail a hand over the soft space between high, pointed ears, scratching lightly. Rufus' tail tries to pound through the floor.

"Do you want coffee, water, or orange juice with your aspirin?"

I glance at Beckett, feeling a damnable flush in my cheeks. "Um. Water, then coffee, but I can—"

"Stop," he says lightly, already turning away. "Sit at the table. Try to relax. And I'll try to ignore how you look in my clothes."

I suck in a breath, blood surging low in my body. "I'm sorry about last night," I say quickly. "I don't remember everything, but I do remember making an ass out of myself."

He glances up from pouring coffee, his smile wicked. "I'm not sorry. You were adorable."

Blushing harder, I make it to the kitchen table and sink into a chair. Rufus follows, his warm head dropping onto my lap. I pet him absentmindedly as Beckett brings me coffee, a glass of water, and two white pills.

I take the aspirin, praying for speedy headache relief, then cradle the mug of coffee. By the time the contents are half-finished, there's a plate of bacon, eggs, and toast in front of me. Beckett joins me with his own serving, tucking in to his meal like this is a perfectly normal situation. Sunday breakfast with me.

"Foods getting cold," he says lightly.

I set down my coffee and take a bite of bacon. The second it hits my palette, I'm starving. An embarrassingly short time later, I sit back with a sigh.

"So good, thank you."

He winks and clears our plates, then refills our coffees and settles back into his chair. We stare at each other over our mugs. *I'm sitting at his kitchen table. In his clothes. Like we're a couple.* The thoughts ping harmoniously and contentment surges in my chest.

"Do you have plans today?" he asks at length.

"No," I wheeze.

He smiles. "Is there anything you'd like to do?"

Besides you?

"Um, nothing in particular."

"Great," he says decisively. "Then I'm teaching you how to play chess."

My brows shoot up. "Chess?"

He chuckles. "You really don't remember much, do you? You were enamored of my custom chess set last night. You told me you've always wanted to play but never learned because you knew initially you'd lose."

I blanch. "What else did I tell you?" I ask, thinking about the letters. His gaze lowers, a small, private smile on his lips. "James! Put me out of my misery. What did I say?"

"You might have mentioned that my accent turns you on." Smile falling, his eyes lift to mine; the look in them makes me shiver. "And that you write me letters every night. And miss me teasing you. Touching you. Do you, Iris? Miss me?"

I swallow thickly. "Yes," I breathe, then shake my head. "But nothing's changed—"

"I know," he says mutedly. "You're still my student, and I'm still married. Julia finally signed the papers, though, so the last bit will be remedied shortly."

The air gusts from my lungs. "Oh. Well, that's good. Congratulations?"

"Thanks." He huffs in soundless laughter, dragging a hand through his hair. It's been cut recently, but the strands are still long enough to grab.

I squirm in my seat, the friction inadvertently spiking my arousal even higher.

His eyes narrow, a smile curving his lips. "You're blushing. What are you thinking about?"

My pulse pounds harder. Need for him rises, unraveling my control faster than I can rebuild it.

This is a mistake. Don't—

"I need a shower," says my traitorous mouth. "Do you want to join me?" His fingers spasm on his coffee mug, almost dropping it.

"Yes," he says tightly, "but not if you're going to panic after and shut me out. It was devastating the first time."

I carefully set my mug on the table. "Okay, but I have a condition, too."

His eyes flare hungrily. "Yes?"

"No talking about the future. No thinking about tomorrow. Just be with me today. Can we do that? Be together today?"

He studies me a long moment. "What if I want more than today?"

My heart squeezes, but I ignore it. "Tomorrow isn't

on the table right now. But I want you. Your hands and mouth on me. Now. Is that enough?"

He uncoils to standing, veering around the table. I take his extended hand and he draws me to my feet. Fingertips whisper around my throat, sinking into the hair at my nape. He lifts my face toward his, tugging me forward until we're chest to chest.

Dark with desire, his eyes fly across my face. "My answer is yes. I am your willing servant, begging for scraps from your table."

My eyes flutter closed. "More," I whisper.

Lips graze my forehead. "I dream every day about being inside you again. Feeling your sweet body milk me dry, hearing your little whimpers in my ear. I imagine in lurid detail all the things I want to do to you. With you. I want your legs around my neck as you ride my face. And forgive me, but I *really* fucking want my cock in your mouth."

A small, helpless sound escapes me and my knees weaken. He catches me, hoisting me into his arms. I wrap myself around him, tucking my face into his warm neck as he heads for the stairs.

"It's the accent, isn't it?" he asks cheekily.

I laugh breathlessly and nip at his throat. "Probably. But there's a chance your talents are being wasted on crime fiction."

He hums in humor, hands skating under my shirt to find skin. For the briefest moment, I worry about the scars. Then he says, "The only erotica I'll write will be for you. Tomes and tomes of it, my little muse."

I forget the scars.

I forget everything but him.

14. conceit

I'll never look at a detachable showerhead the same way again. Or bathroom counters. And I'll never forget the look on James' face as he undressed me before the mirrors, forcing me see myself through his eyes. Every imperfect part of me was made perfect, first by his gaze, then his hands, and finally his mouth. Every slick scar, narrow or thick. Every swirled crease of the burns on my side.

He worshipped them all.

We didn't even make it to the shower, the first time. He took me from behind, my hands gripping the countertop, my body exposed to daylight and mirrors. Each time it became too much and I closed my eyes, he begged me to open them, coaxing with hands and words until finally, that sweet darkness swept away my fear.

I embraced the sight of our bodies together, allowing myself to accept the truth in his eyes. His lack of revulsion or pity. His passion and tenderness, and a need so vast it's both freeing and terrifying.

Over the next hours, he keeps his promise to not speak of the future. Even when we finally make it to the bed, and the sharp edge of passion melts into something infinitely softer and deeper.

Face to face, our breaths mingle as our bodies surge together in perfect concert. My legs around his hips, my fingers on his waist, I watch his beautiful face in wonder as he finds release. And for a moment his eyes reflect the words he wants to say, but I shake my head, pressing my face to his throat until the moment passes.

We sleep for a time, curled tightly together, but eventually Rufus' whining outside the bedroom rouses us.

"He's going to the pound."

I cuddle into his chest, laughing soundlessly. "He's probably hungry." My stomach growls loudly. "Oh wait, that's me."

He chuckles and presses a kiss to my forehead. "Me, too. Lord, what time is it? I feel like we're in a vortex."

Turning in his arms, I look out the window to see a sky dark with clouds. "Sometime between noon and six p.m., I'd say." Stretching languorously, I shimmy back into his heat.

He thrusts against the curve of my ass, stirring slightly. "Poor boy can't keep up with his lady's demand," he whispers into my shoulder.

Rufus' whining intensifies.

"Saved by the dog," I say, turning to smile at him.

He kisses my nose. "I'll take him for a quick walk. But only if you promise you won't do something rash like sneak out when I'm gone."

I yawn. "That sounds exhausting. I'll make us something to eat instead. And by that I mean, where do you keep your delivery menus?"

He chuckles. "Kitchen drawer closest to the living room. I'll leave my cell and card on the counter." With a final kiss, he scoots off the bed and walks naked across the room to his dresser.

Not until he says my name twice do I look up and see his smug grin. I shrug. "You have a spectacular ass."

He shakes his head chidingly, but his eyes sparkle as he tosses clothes in my direction. "I was going to offer you some boxers, but I've changed my mind. No underwear for you."

I comply without resistance, and when man and dog are gone, I dress. Another pair of drawstring pants and a soft, long-sleeved shirt that I know he picked for its thinness. Glancing at myself in the full length mirror, I smirk at the clear outlines of my breasts and nipples.

"Prick," I whisper affectionately, and head downstairs to find the menus.

The afternoon passes like a dream. We feed each other Chinese food and share the gelato I spied in his freezer. As the storm outside progresses, we light candles and a fire and snuggle together on the couch.

We chat about inconsequential things. Countries and landmarks I want to visit (most of which he's seen), the last book we read (Neil Gaiman's newest for both of us), and what superpower we'd like to have. He chooses teleportation, and I decide on being able to speak all languages.

At length, he sets up the chessboard with its beautifully handcrafted pieces on the coffee table. He then patiently teaches me the fundamentals of the game, which I barely absorb because I can't stop staring at his mouth.

We play a few times; I lose.

"Checkmate," he says, smirking. "You haven't learned a thing, have you?"

"Nope," I admit, leaning into the corner of the couch and traveling my foot up his thigh. He catches it before I make it to his crotch. Grabbing my other foot from the floor, he draws them both into his lap.

I relax, thinking I'm about to enjoy a foot massage. The next thing I know, he's mercilessly tickling the soles of my feet, and I'm laughing so hard I'm crying, shrieking, "Stop, stop! I'm going to pee my freaking pants!"

When he finally takes pity on me, it's only because he's laughing too hard to continue. I throw a couch pillow at him. He tosses it away and hauls me into his lap. Straddling him, looking down at his grinning face, I'm reminded of a detail from our first and only bout of cybersex.

I whip my shirt off. His grin sharpens, arms flexing to draw my breasts toward his mouth. His tongue flicks one nipple, then the other, and his breathing deepens.

"Exactly where I want them," he murmurs, gaze rising to my face. "I don't want you to leave. Ever."

Warmth surges in my heart, spreading fast to my belly and lower. I trace his lips with my index finger.

"I know, but after this you're taking me home. And you'll have to wait a whole week to have me again."

He stills, eyes bright. "Sundays?"

Biting my lip, I whisper, "Okay?"

His smile is all the answer I need.

*P*ouring rain provides sufficient cover for my walk of shame—only I don't feel any shame, just deep and abiding contentment.

After a last, lingering kiss that I feel all the way to my toes, I lift his borrowed raincoat over my head and run into my building. Thankfully, there's no one around to see me wearing men's pajamas and emerald green ballet flats, carrying a rumpled Halloween costume under my arm.

Having texted Claire ahead of time to make sure she's home, my knock is answered almost immediately. When we're inside, she looks me up and down, smiling and shaking her head. I grin sheepishly and she finally laughs, pulling me into tight hug.

"Harlot," she says happily. "Tell me everything."

I flop onto the couch. "I'm still processing. But holy hell, Claire, he's *experienced.*"

She giggles. "I knew it! And I'm so glad, I can't even tell you." She drops to the cushion next to me, her smile slowly fading. "I don't want to be a downer, but there's something you need to know."

Heartbeat tripping, I sit up. "What?"

She winces. "Someone saw you walking together to his car. Holding hands."

My stomach nosedives. "Who?"

"Griff heard it from Kirk, who heard it from someone else. I think it was a faculty member. Maggie Something-or-Other?"

Dread crystallizes. "No," I whisper, grabbing fistfuls of my hair. "No no no! Where's my phone?"

The sympathy on Claire's face is overwhelming. "Plugged in by the coffee maker." I jolt to my feet and beeline for the kitchen. Claire follows. "Before I forget, I talked to your mom this morning. I told her you were in the shower and would call her back."

"Thanks," I say distractedly, grabbing my phone.

The first thing I see is a text from James.

Maggie saw us—I'll take care of it

Claire peers over my shoulders. "Oh, well that's good, right?"

I laugh humorlessly. "Not really. My entire academic career in the hands of one of his ex-lovers."

Claire sums up my emotional state with a succinct, "Ugh."

I don't write James back, too sharp-edged at the moment to say anything remotely positive. Instead, I toss down the phone and scrub my face with my hands. As the situation sets in, panic cycles in prickly waves through my chest.

Then Claire asks softly, "It was worth it, though, wasn't it?"

Memories of the day rise in a bright collage. His breathless moans as I fulfilled his carnal wish for my mouth on him. Fingers teasing my hair and skin as we lay curled together in bed. His debauched imagination, his salacious whispers in my ear. Learning the different languages of his laughter and smiles. The way his eyes lit up when I rolled on the living room floor with Rufus, scratching his belly until his legs twitched.

My anxiety melts away.

I look at Claire through my fingers. "So worth it. But I'm *so* sore."

She laughs in delight. "I'll bet. Oh honey, I'm so happy for you. Not just because you got laid. You *look* happy. Glowing. And in the scheme of things, no one gives a shit. Professors and grad students getting together is the worst kept secret in history."

I grimace. "You're probably right, but it could still make the next eight months of my life torture. If it blows up, what professor is going to want to write me a recommendation? Ack, I can't even think about it."

"Don't. Just enjoy the afterglow." Giving me another hug, she says, "I have some reading to do. Don't forget to call your mom back, okay?"

"I won't. Thanks, Claire. By the way, what was the cover story you gave Griffen and Brad?"

She pauses at the kitchen door and winks. "Aunt Flo, of course."

I laugh. When she's gone, I pour myself a glass of water and wander into my bedroom to call my mom. She doesn't answer, so I leave a voicemail apologizing for missing her. And asking if we can move our call day to Saturdays.

Sundays belong to James.

I shower almost regretfully, washing traces of our final union from my skin. After drying off and pulling on pajamas, I throw his clothes in my hamper. Then I change my mind and grab the shirt, tossing it near my pillow.

Once in bed, I open my laptop and review my assignment calendar for the week, but the words quickly blur. Even though it's barely nine o'clock, I power down my computer, turn off the bedside light, and snuggle under the covers with my phone.

His shirt tucked under my cheek, I text him.

I miss you

I wait a few minutes for a reply, but my heavy eyelids close before it comes.

My heart pounding nervously, I open the classroom door. The head of the room is empty, though most of the students are already inside. After trading greetings, I claim my desk and pull out my phone, bringing up the text message I received this morning.

Sent at 12:01 a.m., it reads, **Six days is 144 hours too long.** I'm still smiling at the words when the door opens and James strides into the room.

"Good morning," he says, dropping his bag on the desk and facing the class. His eyes rest only briefly on my face, but the contact sizzles like a brand. "Who's up for a field trip today?"

The class murmurs enthusiastically.

"Where to, boss?" asks Terrance.

James nods out the window. "Based on the painfully stale content of last week's journals, I'm thinking some fresh air is in order. Sun's out and winter's beauty abounds."

Groans mix with laughter. Molly raises her hand shyly, then blushes when James nods at her. "Do you want us to spend the time journaling, or just reflecting?"

His gaze snaps to me. "What do you think, Ms. Eliot?"

I clear my throat. "With short stories due next week for midterms, I would strongly suggest taking advantage of the time to reflect on your drafts in a new setting. Maybe read them aloud to another classmate."

"In public?" whispers Molly.

Terrance says, "You can read to me, Molls."

James smiles slightly. "Exposure and vulnerability are integral parts of being a writer. Good idea, Ms. Eliot. Everyone team up and head outside. Find a place swarming with people and read your stories to your partner. Loudly."

More groans, but they do as he says, packing up and pairing off. When the classroom is empty, I ask suspiciously, "Do I sense ulterior motives, professor?"

Chuckling, he strolls toward me and sits at the desk beside mine. "Perhaps," he murmurs. "I did want to talk to you about a few things."

His gaze drops from mine and I stiffen. "Such as?" I ask softly.

"I wanted to give you advanced warning. I gave you a low B on your short story. The word count was low, and I thought the antagonist lacked depth. I'm sorry, I know you wrote it the week of your father's death, but—"

My relieved laughter halts him. "James, it wasn't A-material. Don't worry about it."

He sighs, tension releasing from his shoulders. "I thought you were worried about your GPA. God, I felt horrible."

I reach forward and grab his hand, squeezing it tightly. "Stop. We can't go down this road. And no one cares about GPA at this point. They care about letters of recommendation and writing portfolios."

He nods, but frowns slightly. "I thought you wanted a PhD."

My skin tingles. "How do you know that?"

"You told me Saturday night," he says gently. "The promise to Derrick."

Squeezing my eyes closed, I wait for shock to fade. I take a deep breath. Then another one, until the world levels out again.

"Sorry, I, uh, don't remember telling you that," I finally say, opening my eyes to his intent gaze. "I promised Derrick I would go past a Bachelors, that's it. Sure, we joked about me being Dr. Eliot—like people assuming I could do surgery when really I'm just awesome at writing papers—but a PhD isn't on the table for me."

"Why not? What's stopping you?"

I take another deep breath to overcome the impulse to snap at him. None of my feelings about school are his fault or responsibility.

"Life. Just life. We're talking at least three more years of school and adding tens of thousands to my already substantial loans." I smirk. "Maybe I'd rather go your route. Get published and famous."

He smiles, but his eyes stay somber. "I know you'll accomplish absolutely anything you put your mind to." After a small hesitation, he asks, "Have you given any more thought to the memorial?"

I blink in stupefaction. "Is there anything I *didn't* drunkenly confess Saturday night?"

He chuckles. "Doubtlessly. Are you going?"

I pause, then nod. "Yeah. My mom sent me an email this morning with the details. It's next Saturday in Monterey." I shake my head in delayed disbelief. "Apparently his will specified that he wanted his ashes scattered at this little beach near the church they were married in. I'm not sure how to feel about that."

"He loved her very much," says James, and when I frown at him, he clarifies, "Obviously, given his last wishes."

I study him a moment. "Did you know him well?"

He shrugs. "As well as any other student, I suppose. Dr. Eliot was a legend—former Poet Laureate, recipient of innumerable honors, with a reputation for shaping the careers of young writers. He was one of the main reasons I wanted to study literature at Stanford. He was a brilliant teacher but a tough one. I seem to remember an odd preoccupation with semi-colons."

"He hated them," I murmur.

James smiles, nodding. "I took every course and seminar he taught and worked my ass off for him to notice me. One of my finest moments was when he pulled me aside senior year and told me to apply for the Stegner Fellowship."

In lieu of a graduate level Creative Writing Program, Stanford offers the highly respected working artists' fellowship. From my obsessive pre-term Googling, I know James didn't complete the fellowship, but I ask, "Did you apply?"

He shakes his head. "My book of poetry was about to be published, and I'd just completed my first novel."

"And the rest is history," I say with a smile.

He did, in fact, continue his schooling at Stanford,

earning a Masters in English Literature and starting the subsequent PhD program, though he withdrew after a year.

By then, though, he'd been sitting pretty on the New York Times Bestsellers list and had snagged a lucrative publishing contract at the ripe old age of twenty-five.

Watching my face carefully, he says, "You should know, I was invited to the memorial."

"*What?* Why?"

He shrugs, visibly discomfited. "Richard and I corresponded occasionally over the years. Nothing in depth until, uh, recently. In the spirit of full disclosure, Iris, your father wanted me to write the forward for a book of poems he was publishing."

My breath whistles through my teeth. "Wow. Right up till the end, he was a selfish ass. I'm sorry, James, but he likely just wanted to capitalize on your fame."

He nods solemnly. "I'm well aware."

"Are you going?" I ask haltingly.

"Only if you want me to."

I tilt my head consideringly, letting him sweat a minute. "Only if we fly down together and share a hotel room."

His eyes widen, then narrow, sparkling with mischief. "You little minx. You want to make a holiday for us out of your father's funeral weekend? I'm aghast."

I roll my eyes. "It's a miracle I'm going at all. The man was basically a stranger. So, what do you say? King-sized bed, room service, and minibars? Or a Sunday without me?"

He smiles slowly. "One condition."

"Yes?"

"My treat."

I consider whether or not to be offended long enough to realize I don't care. "Deal."

He snatches my hand, bringing my knuckles to his lips. "I rather like this new, less combative you."

I snort, then sober. "Speaking of combative, what happened with Maggie?"

With a final kiss, he releases my hand. "You can be assured that by the end of our conversation, she wasn't sure *what* or *who* she actually saw."

"Really? How did you manage that?"

He cocks a brow. "The accent, naturally."

I kick his shoe. "As long as she doesn't want proof—like *physical* proof..."

"Not an option," he says, then smiles wickedly. "Before I forget, how are you feeling today? You seem a tad uncomfortable in that hard chair."

Blushing, I kick his foot harder. "You're incorrigible."

"Mmm," he agrees. "Insatiable, too, thanks to my

little muse. I had a delicious dream last night about a white-sand beach. You were wearing this indecent bikini and were covered in body oil. I had to take an extra-long shower this morning—"

The classroom door opens and Molly and Terrance walk into the room. By the time they notice us, I'm pretending to type while James points at my screen.

"That sentence there needs reworking." He looks up at the students. "Back so soon? How'd it go?"

I dance my fingers on the keyboard, staring at the dark screen and trying my damnedest not to laugh.

16. deconstruction

By Saturday afternoon, I can't wait any longer. Four days of keeping our distance on campus, plus four nights of long phone calls with barely restrained carnal undertones, have rendered me powerless over my need for James Beckett. After a quick text to confirm he's home, I pack a small bag and call a cab.

The front door opens before I'm even out of the car. James stands on the threshold, mouthwateringly shirtless as he holds Rufus by the collar. I rush into the house. The second the door closes, my bag hits the floor and I'm in his arms.

Between kisses and stumbling progress to his bedroom, I mumble, "Sorry Rufus, we'll play soon. I need to greet your daddy first." James chuckles, maneuvering us into the bedroom and shutting the door before Rufus can follow.

A piteous whine sounds.

"He'll live," says James, and we fall onto the bed.

My clothes are quickly discarded, tossed haphazardly around the room. A shoe hits a wall. My jeans lasso a floor lamp. I yank his soft pants from his hips and eagerly reach for him. He groans, cock swelling in my fists.

"I want you," he whispers against my neck.

I arch beneath him, wrapping my legs around his hips. "I know," I answer, dragging the tip of him through my wetness, torturing us both with the temptation of nothing between us. "Do you feel that? What you do to me?"

He grunts, angling a hand between us to sink two fingers inside me. His mouth drops to my breast, tongue swirling around my nipple as his hand builds a shattering rhythm. When his thumb joins, smoothing in steady circles over my clit, I turn my head to bite a pillow.

"Iris, sweet Iris, it's become my mission in life to make you scream."

When he replaces his thumb with his mouth, I do scream—a ragged cry of surrender. My vision brightens, my body humming at higher and higher frequency. And just when I think I can't possibly feel *more,* I look down and see his eyes on me.

The climax doesn't build—it explodes. I throw my head back and give myself over, again and again, until there's nothing left to give. Slowly, his fingers and tongue retreat, and he rains kisses across my center.

As I twitch and relearn how to breathe, he says lightly, "I would happily stay here all day, love, but if you want me to move, I need my hair back."

I unclench my fingers at last and he lifts his head. "Not sorry," I tell him.

He laughs, rising to settle back on his heels. My post-orgasm sedation fades beneath a fresh wave of need. I sit up and reach for him, determined to return the favor, but he grabs my arms and lifts me up. Seated on his thighs with my legs draped to either side of him, he palms my ass and tugs me closer.

"This was the image in my mind," he murmurs, "What I was trying to type. One-handed."

Arms around his shoulders, I roll my hips. "Like this?" I whisper. "You want me to ride you, James?"

His teeth clench, eyes closing tightly. "Condom, right now. Or I'm going to do something stupid."

I scramble across the bed, yanking open a small drawer, and carefully tear the packet open. The next moments aren't graceful, but together we get the condom on. Then I'm back where I started. His whole body trembles beneath mine.

"Take me," he whispers.

I don't hesitate. He's already at my entrance, so I rock myself onto him, pausing to adjust to each new level of fullness. When he can't stand it anymore, he grabs me hard, meeting my next thrust with one that buries him completely. The angle is beyond consuming, more than pleasure. I still, gasping into his mouth.

"Okay?" he whispers.

I roll my hips experimentally. Fiery sensation expands through my limbs. "Oh, yes," I answer, and find the rhythm my body wants. *Needs.* "More than okay."

As I move, strong hands roam up my back, through my hair, and down to grip my hips. Mouth angled to my ear, he whispers, "This feeling, right here and now, has brought gods from their heavenly thrones, started and ended wars, and shifted the borders of nations. Nothing in my life has prepared me for how you make me feel, Iris."

I shudder, finding his mouth with mine to stall further words. Because the ones he's already spoken are too much, too powerful—they're everything I've always longed to hear and didn't believe could be possible for me.

So I deny my heart's desire to join my words to his

and instead increase my body's rhythm. I take him, just like he asked, until his tenderness shifts to the sharper edge of passion. Pushing off his heels, he lowers me to the bed, yanking my legs around his waist.

From there, the only language we speak is wordless.

*W*hile James takes Rufus for a walk, I wander downstairs perusing bookshelves and peeking into closed rooms. When I find his study, I can't resist the temptation of a glimpse inside his writer's mind.

The room is spare—nothing on the walls, no furniture save a small couch, bookshelf, and a desk, the latter's surface empty except for a closed laptop and his slim journal.

On the bookshelf, instead of books there are tens of journals, dates scrawled on the slim white spines. I run a finger across a row, tracing the chronological order, seeing dates from this year.

Despite the temptation to pull one free, I let my hand fall and instead move to the desk, grazing my palm over the cool laptop. Tucked beneath the computer are post-it notes filled with his slanted scrawl. One of them peeks out, and before I can turn away, I see my name.

Iris Eliot
2004

Will Cabot–

Colombia Law,
graduated 2013.

Shock explodes, shooting icy needles through every inch of me. I hear a small sound like that of a wounded animal, but don't immediately realize it's from me.

Will Cabot is the name of the boy I thought I loved. The boy who, after four months of dating, decided he didn't want to wait for my consent to have sex with me.

My arm shoves the laptop aside, exposing a series of notes.

Richard wrote her
letters every
holiday, birthday—
always returned to
sender.

Find out about
scars, how bad—
why no plastic
surgery? —Richard
offered.

Writer like father.
Pursuing PhD?

Novels not poetry,
too close?

Never pressed
charges for assault.

No longterm
relationships—

PTSD?

"Oh my God," I whisper.

There are others, but the words blur into streams of black. My breathing is loud and ragged. I can't feel my lips. My chest feels heavy, and inside it... a steel hammer pounds steadily into my heart, grinding it to dust.

Everything he's ever said to me has been a lie. *Everything.*

"Iris." My name is a horrified gasp. "Let me explain."

Rufus pushes against my side, warm and solid, his nose digging affectionately into my hip. I carefully slide the laptop back and turn, tucking my freezing hands into my armpits. *Why are my teeth chattering?* The question floats through me and away.

"You're writing a book about me," I whisper, staring at his chest because I can't look at his face.

"No," he says desperately. "It's about your father. It's just research, please. God, you were never supposed to see that."

Panic cleaves me in two.

Adrenaline surges into the void.

Unsafe. Not safe. Run.

Obeying my body's command, I shove past him, tearing up the stairs and slamming the bedroom door behind me. I make sure it's locked, then scramble in my bag for my phone. Hands shaking, I almost dial Claire. But she doesn't have a car, and I can't handle her asking Griffen to get me. So I dial the only relative I have in the state.

Miraculously, Allison answers. "Iris! How are you?"

My voice comes on the third try. "Ally, I-I'm really

sorry to ask this. But it's kind of 911. Can you come get me?"

"Absolutely. Are you okay? Where are you?"

I tell her the address. "I'm okay. Physically, at least. How far away are you?"

"I'm just leaving work. I'll be there in under ten."

"Thank you," I whisper, and disconnect.

When I crack open the bedroom door, the hallway is empty. Downstairs, Rufus tackles a squeaky toy; I hear thumps and happy barks, but nothing else.

One step at a time. Go.

I walk down the stairs, numb and robotic, made of cold metal parts. As the living room becomes visible, I see James sitting on the couch. His back is to me, his head braced in his hands.

Walk outside. You can do it.

My footstep creaks on the final step and I freeze. Rufus looks up from his toy, ears perking excitedly as he sees me.

"Sit," says James sharply. Whining, Rufus lowers to his haunches. "Do you need cab fare?"

Brokenness rises, a searing storm. "I don't need anything from you," I snarl.

The muscles in his back tighten. "For what it's worth, I was going to tell you. I just didn't know how."

"Tell me *what?*" I ask with rising volume. "That you

plan on telling the world how a stupid girl got her brother killed and nearly died herself?"

James drags hands through his hair and laces his fingers tightly at the back of his neck. "No. Yes. *Fuck*. It's a biography. I couldn't leave you out of it. The accident... it changed Richard. His life, his writing—"

A sudden epiphany rocks me on my heels. "This was *his* idea, wasn't it? Motherfucking Father of the Year, Richard Eliot. Ruining my life from beyond the grave."

James rockets to his feet, spinning toward me. "He tried to *help* you, Iris! A thousand times. I've read every letter he sent you that you returned unopened. He told me about the times he tracked you down, begged you to see him. To talk to him. He wanted to pay for your schooling, for reconstructive surgery, for therapy. You shut him out!"

I shake my head slowly, finally meeting his gaze. "Richard Eliot walked away from his family because he wanted girlfriends more than he wanted us."

"That's not true," he seethes. "Your mother was the one who had the affair. It tore their marriage apart."

Like a physical blow, the words catch me in the stomach. I clutch my middle, gasping for air.

"You're lying," I gasp.

Regret swiftly replaces his anger. "Iris—"

"No!" I yell. "Fuck you, James. Or should I say

congratulations? You can now write about my scars with firsthand knowledge. Don't forget to include my long-standing habit of falling for men who use and discard me. Chalk it up to my—apparently misguided—daddy complex."

My phone buzzes in my hand, and a second later a car honks outside. I meet James' tortured eyes and feel nothing. No sorrow, no attraction, no betrayal, no love.

"Since you're such an expert on my father, you should know he left everything to me. If you write any of that shit about me or my mother, I'll use all his money to bury you in lawsuits for the next twenty years. I'll tell everyone who will listen that you seduced me—*your student*—as a means of researching your book. We'll see how long it takes for your publishing company to drop you, your agent to fire you, and every university in the country to blacklist you."

Lips thinned, James nods sharply. "Can't say I blame you, Iris. But I'm writing it anyway."

The final, untouched piece of my heart drops into darkness.

"I hate you," I breathe.

He flinches, then smiles sadly. "As you should. But until you read it, may some small part of you know that I never lied about my feelings for you. From the moment I saw you, I've been yours. Mind, body, and heart."

My sight blurs with tears. "Fuck you," I whisper, and flee across the living room, out the front door, and down the steps.

As I hit the walkway, my knee twinges—almost gives out—but I ignore it, limp-running to the car at the curb. I yank open the passenger door and tumble inside.

"Go, go, please," I chant, turning terrorized eyes on Allison.

She hits the gas.

17. denouement

I stare at the stained glass windows high above the altar in Stanford Memorial Church. The pews behind us are packed with students, faculty, and staff of the university. At the lectern, the dean speaks of my father's time at Stanford. I hear words like *honor* and *kindness* and *loved* and my fingernails dig half-moons in my palms.

"Iris, baby, are you sure you want to be here?"

I don't reply to the worried whisper, because the only answer I can give would require me running down the central aisle screaming at the top of my lungs.

My poor mom probably thinks I'm overcome by grief. Either that or seconds from the psychiatric ward. I've barely spoken to her since flying down Monday after hastily informing my professors that I would, in fact, be taking a week's bereavement. Phillip and my sister Victoria have likewise welcomed me with open arms. Like Allison, they insist on worming their way into my heart through unfailing acceptance and sympathy.

It's not their fault I can't muster the decency to return their affection. The problem is my brokenness, which no amount of kindness can fix.

Since Saturday, I haven't felt... right. Like everything decent, hopeful, and good in me switched off when I read that first post-it note. This is the first time I've left the family's palatial Palo Alto home since arriving; I've spent most of the week holed up in a guest bedroom. When I'm not sleeping, I'm writing, and when I can't sleep or write, I numb my brain with television.

Not until this morning, when I saw the brochure for the public memorial at Stanford, had I considered accompanying my mom. The actual funeral isn't until tomorrow, and truly, I'd rather be swimming with sharks at the moment, but there'd been a name listed under the contributors to the service.

James S. Beckett.

The knowledge that he changed his plane ticket, arriving a day early in order to speak on my father's behalf, had so incensed me that I'd told my mother to wait for me as I dressed.

At the lectern, the dean wraps up his speech with,

"Please welcome internationally acclaimed author, Stanford alum, and a close friend of Dr. Eliot's, Mr. James Beckett."

As James takes the dean's place at the lectern, there's a wave of murmuring from the back of the church where the bulk of the students sit. Like my father, James is a legend here.

In a tailored black suit and crimson university tie, his dark hair only marginally tamed, he looks exactly like the forbidden fantasy of coeds. Alluring and a little wild. Deviant and brilliant.

I fucking hate him.

And I still want him. So badly that even now, arousal stirs low in my belly.

Damnit.

"I first met Dr. Eliot as a freshman…"

My mom leans close to whisper, "Isn't he—"

"Yes," I hiss. "My professor."

She sits back, a thoughtful look on her face as James tells the congregation several anecdotes that trigger laughter. His answering wry smiles twist the knife in my heart to unbearable levels; I stare down at my clenched hands.

"…many of you know, Richard was a complex man." More knowing laughter. "When he was working on a poem, he was temperamental, contentious, and often unreasonable. Especially when a student asked for an extension." More laughter.

His voice softens, becoming solemn. "And yet, there was little in the world he loved more than teaching. Poetry itself, perhaps. But his greatest love of all was his family, who we're honored to have with us today."

My head whips up in time to see him gesture at my mom and me. He meets my frigid stare with a sad smile, then looks back at the congregation.

"I've had the recent honor of teaching Richard's daughter, Iris, at the University of Washington. A novelist of incredible promise, Iris is a testament to Richard's legacy. His talent, his mark on the world, lives on in her."

Son of a bitch.

It's a miracle I don't yell the words. Instead, I jerk to my feet, eliciting startled whispers and a horrified gasp from my mother. Head down, I move carefully past the others in the row, then walk down the red-carpeted aisle toward the distant doors.

Hundreds of eyes follow me.

James' voice reaches my ears as I cross the empty antechamber. "...just as brilliant and complex as her father."

I push open the doors a little harder than necessary and walk into the blinding sunshine.

fter a tense drive home—in which my mom asks me what happened and I tell her I don't want to talk about it—I borrow her car and go for a drive.

I don't truly contemplate where I'm going until an hour-and-a-half later, when I hit the coast of Monterey and a tiny, familiar parking lot. Several blocks behind me is the church my parents were married in, and tomorrow, the small, windswept cove is where we'll scatter my father's ashes.

I walk onto the damp sand and sit. Alone in the cold, I stare at the ocean long enough for the sun to drop below the horizon, for the temperature to dive. I don't feel it.

I don't feel anything.

When a car door slams behind me, I close my eyes and prepare to tell my mother everything. To demand the answers I want. But it isn't her voice that comes softly to my ears.

"I had a feeling you'd be here, love."

I laugh bitterly. "Don't call me that. You may think you know me, James, but you don't. Leave me the fuck alone."

Instead, a warm coat falls around my shoulders. I

grab it, intending to throw it to the sand, but before I can, he sits behind me and wraps me in his arms.

"Let me *go*," I say through my teeth.

"No," he whispers.

I buck, but there's no power in it. I'm half-frozen, famished, and haven't slept without nightmares for a week.

"Why are you doing this?" I ask shrilly. "I don't want you here. I don't *want* you."

"I know," he says against my hair. "But I'm a prick, so I don't give a damn. You may think you're hiding it well, but I can see your pain. And I want you to know you're not alone."

"Fuck you," I snarl.

"Mmm, if you'd like," he murmurs impudently. "My hotel's not far."

I laugh hoarsely. "Drop the act. You got what you wanted."

He makes a pained noise. "I know I lied to you and that you'll likely never forgive me. But I never lied about wanting you. I still want you. So much."

From my broken place comes the words, "If I keep sleeping with you, will you leave my mom out of the book?"

He goes very, very still. "You really don't trust me at all, do you? Not even after everything we've shared? You think I wouldn't use every ounce of diplomacy I possess to tell their story? That I wouldn't do my utmost to be impartial?"

I twist in his arms, searching his shadowed face. "No, I don't. I don't think you're impartial, having only heard my father's side." I shove his arms away from me. "And what about Will Cabot? Are you going to talk about him, too? *Impartially?* For a stupid decision he made as a teenager and the guilt he lives with for the accident?"

James reels backward in shock. "Are you bloody serious? He raped you, Iris, and got off scot-free when you wouldn't press charges."

I climb unsteadily to my feet. "You don't know what you're talking about. Get your facts straight, asshole. Yes, he roofied me, but Derrick showed up before anything happened. And Will came to me later and apologized, and told me he wasn't going to go through with it. That when Derrick burst in, he was trying to get me dressed."

James doesn't say anything for a long time. Then he stands, brushes off his slacks, and retrieves his blazer from the ground. Before I can surmise his intent, he steps close and cups my face, thumb brushing across my cold cheek.

"I'm so sorry, love," he whispers. "If you ever need me, all you have to do is call. Goodbye, my little muse."

Then he's gone, striding toward the parking lot. I

wait until he pulls away before walking stiffly to my mom's car and getting inside. Turning on the engine, I huddle in driver's seat as heat blasts from the vents. As my body thaws, it begins to shake violently. Misery claws through me, expelling in a strangled scream.

I see James' handwriting on yellow post-it notes.

Never pressed charges for assault.

Not attempted assault.

Assault.

No long-term relationships—PTSD?

"From the accident," I whisper. "PTSD from the accident."

Dropping my head to the steering well, I think back to that night, digging past the hazy memories of that fateful drive. I remember... whispering. Laughing. I remember... suffocation. No, not suffocation. Being held down. And voices. More than one.

Just do it, Will.

Don't chicken out.

Okay, okay.

Grab her legs.

Derrick yelling. Fists meeting flesh.

You raped my sister, you piece of shit! You're fucking dead!

Sobbing—my sobbing.

Derrick?

I'm coming, sis. Another punch. *She just saved your life, asshole. Enjoy your final days of freedom, because you're going to jail for a long fucking time.*

Bile rises in my throat. I jerk open the car door in time to vomit my stomach lining onto the asphalt. Between heaves, I whisper a litany of, "No, no, no."

I don't know how much time passes. Seconds. Hours. Eventually the convulsions lessen and fade, and I spit on the ground. I finally feel the effects of winter, my skin rippling with goosebumps under a sheen of cold sweat.

Tires crunch in the parking lot and headlights sweep over me. A car door opens and closes. I hear running footsteps.

"Iris? Baby, are you okay?" My mom's gentle hands draw the hair back from my face. "I was driving here when I got a call from your professor. He said you needed me? What happened, darling?"

I stare into her worried face and ask the question with an answer I never wanted to know.

"I was raped, wasn't I?"

Tears fill her eyes. "Oh, baby girl. You remembered?"

"I-I don't know. Maybe." I grip her wrists tightly. "Tell me. God, please just tell me."

In a shaking voice, she tells me.

"One of the doctors noticed blood. In the prelimi-nary exam, they thought it was your cycle or another injury from the accident. You were in such bad shape. In surgery for hours. But that doctor insisted on a rape kit and blood test. They found..." She chokes back a sob. "Tearing, traces of latex. But no other p-physical evidence. And you tested positive for Rohypnol. Someone came to speak with you a few days later. Do you remember?"

"Vaguely," I whisper.

Her grief-stricken eyes meet mine. "You didn't have any memories of the assault. I was told it was either a side effect of the drugs or post-traumatic amnesia. One of the doctors even said it was a blessing. The night was so hugely traumatic for you, with Derrick..." She stifles another sob with her hand. "Baby, I'm sorry. I'm so very sorry. I'd give anything in the world to take away your pain, then and now. I should have done something."

"You did everything you could, mom," I say. And it's true. There were months and months of sessions with a female psychiatrist, whose leading questions about that night had angered me and eventually distanced me from her help.

I think of the look on James' face as I defended Will. The rage, the dawning horror as he realized I didn't know. All these years, I've believed I lost my virginity to my first college boyfriend.

I'm so sorry, love.

My stomach cramps with another wave of nausea.

"I don't feel good," I mumble. "Don't think I can drive."

"Okay, baby, come here."

She helps me to my feet, then guides me around the car to the passenger side. Once I'm inside with my seat-belt on, she gets behind the wheel.

"What about the other car?" I ask.

"Phillip came with me."

"Oh."

"What do you need right now, baby? Anything? Or just home?"

James...

"Just home, please."

I drop my head back and close my eyes.

18. dissonance

I sleep hard for ten hours. No nightmares or dreams at all. When I wake up the next morning, my mind is clear and sharp. I have breakfast downstairs, and for the first time this week, feel present in my family. Phillip and Victoria bicker about her curfew; she concedes defeat with an eye roll so exaggerated that I smile behind my coffee mug.

Mom serves delicious, misshapen blueberry pancakes. My appetite makes an appearance and I eat a stack of them, plus a pile of strawberries. After, I help with the dishes while outside, Phillip waters rosebushes and upstairs, Victoria blasts pop music in her room.

Closing the loaded dishwasher, I turn to my mom. "What time do we need to leave?"

"The service is at two, so around noon." She pauses,

brushing pale bangs from her eyes. "If you're not feeling up to—"

"I'm going, mom," I interject gently. "And I feel okay. A little weirded out, but honestly, kind of relieved." Sighing, I stare out the kitchen window at the backyard. "I've always felt like something was off. Wrong with me. Something more than just Derrick's death, the accident... At least now it has a name. And I think that doctor was right about it being a blessing. To not remember."

Tears spill down her cheeks as she walks to me and takes my face in her hands. "You're the strongest person I know, Iris. I've always been in awe of you."

"I feel the same away about you, mom," I whisper, even as memory of James' voice filters through my mind.

Your mother was the one who had the affair. It tore their marriage apart.

My stomach sinking, I gently extricate myself and grab my coffee mug. "I'm going to take a shower and maybe write for a bit, okay?"

"Absolutely," she says gently.

Escaping to the guest room, I take a luxuriously long shower. As water beats on the back of my head and neck, intermittent thoughts splash in my mind like paint on a blank canvas. Memories of my father, cast in a new light by James.

Waking up in the hospital to see him sleeping in a chair at my bedside. Returning hundreds of letters from him unopened. Listening to his sobs at Derrick's funeral. And after, turning away as he pounded on the car window begging me to talk to him.

I remember other things, too.

In my freshman year at UW, I heard about a girl who was raped at an off-campus party. I remember the rumors, the scandal. The trial by public opinion. She was drunk, dressed inappropriately. She had a reputation as a party girl. I remember feeling sorry for her.

I also remember Claire telling me when, months after the assault, the girl dropped out and moved home. She never pressed charges. As far as I know, the boy who raped her went on to complete his degree, never suffering any consequences for his actions.

Colombia Law, graduated 2013.

The thought of Will Cabot practicing law ignites a sour blend of disgust and old, stale fear. Is he married? Does he have children? *Is he happy?*

I shiver under the hot water and finally turn off the spray. With a glance at the wall clock, I shelve writing time and get ready for the funeral. Black pants, black blouse, black flats. I carefully do my makeup, covering the shadows beneath my eyes and rubbing color into my pale cheeks. Mascara makes my eyes huge, their darkness even more pronounced.

Selkie-dark.

"Which means you have the eyes of a seal," I tell my reflection. "Not exactly romantic."

Except it was. And is.

Leaving my hair to air dry into its natural waves, I grab my small purse and head downstairs. The sound of voices grows more pronounced as I walk toward the living room, and as though my thoughts conjured him, I hear James' dulcet tones.

I pause on the threshold, heart pounding, and gaze across the room at him. He doesn't see me, his face angled toward my smiling mother. For a moment, longing steals my breath.

Then I remember his betrayal—past and future.

"What the hell are you doing here?" I rasp.

"Iris," gasps my mother, her cheeks coloring in embarrassment. "That's no way to speak to your professor!"

James, looking at me now, cocks a brow. An irreverent smile teases his lips. "Iris, you look lovely. I'm here because your mother agreed to speak with me about her marriage to Richard. Since I'm attending the funeral today and only in town for the weekend, she invited me to accompany you both."

I grip the doorframe, gaze bouncing between them before zeroing in on my mom. "Are you seriously considering this?" I ask bluntly.

"Why wouldn't I?" she asks with surprise. "Your father had a colorful life and I think it's worth telling. Especially by a writer as talented as James."

"Thank you, Mrs. Kirkpatrick," says James.

I sputter, "But you don't know... he thinks you—Gah!"

Spinning, I stalk from the room, through the kitchen, and out the back door. Following a winding path up a small elevation to the pool, I sink onto a padded chaise.

Seconds later, a shadow falls over my legs. "I lied again," he murmurs. "I can easily interview your mother over the telephone. But I wanted to see you."

"You have serious mental problems."

"Undoubtedly."

Not bothering to ask for permission, James sits on the lounge, forcing me to jerk my legs to one side. In the mellow sunlight, the flecks of yellow and blue in his eyes seem to dance. He's too close. *Not close enough.*

"You're like a pimple I can't get rid of," I grumble.

He laughs. "Oh, Iris, how I adore your sass."

Shading my eyes with a hand, I glare at him. "I'm not forgiving you, James. I don't trust you. From the moment we met, you've been lying straight to my face. About knowing who I was, about my accident, about your relationship with my father..." I tilt my head at a sudden thought. "Did you request me as your TA?"

"No," he says softly. "That was the universe having a laugh." He reaches for my other hand, resting near my hip. I snatch it away and he sighs. "Not being upfront with you was a massive error of judgement. The closer we grew, the deeper I seemed to dig myself. And then I couldn't handle the prospect of you loathing me, as I knew you would if you found out about the book."

"Did you come to UW because of me?"

He shakes his head. "Another happy accident, I suppose. Unless you believe in fate."

"I don't," I say quickly.

"I'm not surprised." He smiles softly. "If you want me to leave, I'll make excuses to your mother."

I study his earnest face. "Are you really going to be impartial? What if she says there was no affair?"

He nods thoughtfully. "It had occurred to me. Honestly, I'm not sure how I'd handle that yet, except to present both sides. And anyway, the book isn't focused on his marriage. Or you. It's about him. His childhood in Scotland, his young adult life, and his long career."

I swallow heavily. "You're still not forgiven. Those post-its..." I trail off, unable to articulate the massive shock of reading them.

"I know. It breaks my heart, thinking of the pain you must have felt when you saw them. Will you let me clarify one thing?"

"What?" I ask tensely.

He takes my hand, and this time I don't resist. Trailing fingers along my wrist, he slowly pushes up the sleeve of my blouse to expose several faded white lines.

"These," he says, tracing the scars with his index finger, "are a language of perseverance written on your body. They are indescribably beautiful to me. What you saw on that note—when I wrote that I wondered why you refused cosmetic surgery to lessen their visibility, I hadn't met you. I knew only your father's impressions from after your accident, when your injuries were severe. I'm *glad* you have them. They're a part of you."

"It doesn't matter," I say harshly. But it does. *Goddamnit,* but his words melt a frozen place inside me.

James slowly lowers my sleeve but doesn't release my hand. Lifting it to his lips, he presses a kiss to my knuckles, then to my palm.

"Please, please forgive me," he whispers. "I tried to ignore my desire for you. God, I tried. But I can't help how I feel, and I think—I hope—you feel the same way."

From the back door, my mother calls, "Iris? It's time to go."

"Coming!" I say, then pull my hand away and swing

my legs to the ground opposite him. I can feel the heat of his body on my spine. Too close. *Not close enough.*

And I tell him, "I can't be who you want me to be, James. At sixteen years old, I was broken down to the foundation of my being, and the person who grew up isn't... well."

"That's not true," he says urgently. "You're a kind, sensitive, funny, brilliant woman. There's not a bloody *thing* wrong with you. I've known you six weeks and I'm already—God, you make me feel alive in ways I've never experienced."

I glance back, meeting his stare with effort. "It's just good sex, James. You'll get over it."

He laughs shortly, a burst of aggravation. "Oh, love, you really have no clue. It's not sex with us. And *good* doesn't even scrape the surface of what it is."

I suck in air past a spike of misplaced rage. "You're right. I have no clue, seeing as I lost my virginity to rape and I'm the queen of three-week relationships." I jerk to my feet, ignoring his appalled expression. "Come on, we don't want to be late to my wonderful father's funeral!"

I stalk toward the house. James catches me halfway across the lawn with a hand on my shoulder.

"Stop, Iris. I won't let you do this!"

I whirl and try to shove him, but something misfires in my brain and instead, I find myself grabbing his hair and dragging his face to mine. As our mouths collide, he groans in abject relief, arms locking around me to lift me up and closer.

In the following seconds, nothing exists but the two of us. Our beating hearts, our gasping breaths. The yearning of our bodies and minds, manifesting in the savagery of our kiss.

Then my mother gasps, "Iris! What are you doing?"

I lurch away from James, fingers flying to my swollen lips. He stares at me, hands clenched at his sides, chest heaving.

Broken broken broken.

"I kissed him," I say quickly, turning to face my mom. "It's not his fault."

She nods shortly. "I know, I saw it from the kitchen." Her eyes narrow on James, sparking with maternal indignation. "I saw well enough. Tread carefully, Mr. Beckett. I see how you look at her. And I'll be damned if I stand by and watch you do to her what Richard did to me."

Surprise blooms on his features. He says softly, "I care for your daughter a great deal, Alexandria."

"James," I snap.

My mother's face goes ashen and her gaze swings to me. "Are you in a relationship with your professor? Tell me the truth right now, Iris Mae."

"No, I'm not."

She turns her iciest glare on James. "Perhaps you should travel to the funeral separately, Mr. Beckett." After he nods, she storms inside.

"Now do you believe there are two sides to the story?"

After a small pause, he replies, "Yes."

19. (end) scene

Claire and Griffen pick me up from the airport Sunday night. Emotionally bankrupt from the last few days, I answer their well-meaning questions with monosyllables until they give up trying to reach me.

Once home, I thank them for the ride and escape to my room. And later, alone in bed, I stare sleeplessly at the shadows on the ceiling. I think about my mother, who sobbed while the ashes were scattered yesterday, but mostly I think about the untold story of Richard and Alexandria Eliot.

I know they met in his senior year and her sophomore one at UC Berkeley. He saw her dancing in a university production. He fell in love. Or lust. Either way, he doggedly pursued her over the following year, until she at last succumbed to his charms. Despite his proposal six months later, she made him wait until she graduated to get married.

His poems about her, compiled in the book *Alexandria*, capture a vast range of emotion. Obsession and desire. Love and comfort. They're in turns darkly arresting, gut-wrenching, and achingly sweet. Every one of them is unquestionably masterful.

My mother was an attentive, joyful caretaker to my brother and me. Not once did either of us feel a lack of love. And yet, she's always been a private person; to this day, there are depths to her that I've never dared explore. Memories that remain puzzling. Finding a locked box in her nightstand. Hearing her crying softly in her bedroom while my father was on a book tour.

There was a moment in the car on the way back from the funeral that I almost asked if she'd had an affair. But her pain was so obvious, I couldn't bring myself to add to it. Over the course of the drive, my need became secondary to the blossoming acceptance that whatever happened between her and my father, she loved him as much as he loved her.

And suddenly, I have to know.

Pulling my phone from the nightstand, I call James before I can talk myself out of it. It rings twice.

"Iris," he says softly.

My heart pounding, I ask, "Did she really have an affair?"

He's quiet for several moments. "According to Richard, when Derrick was four and you were one, Alexandria asked your grandmother over one morning to watch you while she ran errands. It wasn't uncommon, but that day she left the house and didn't return. When Richard came home, it was to his worried mother-in-law. As the night wore on, he became more distraught. He drove for hours looking for her but couldn't find her. He called every hospital in the area and even reported her missing. Two days later, she returned. She wouldn't tell him where she'd been and acted like nothing was amiss."

"God," I whisper.

He sighs sadly. "Shortly afterward, Richard found letters in a locked box in her nightstand. They were from her high school sweetheart, and it was clear the man still had feelings for her. Richard confronted her about them, about that weekend. She never denied his accusations. But she never admitted an affair, either."

I don't say anything.

I can't.

Because suddenly, I see the past in a new light. The years of her polite, emotional distance from him at the dinner table. His impassioned bouts of temper behind closed doors. Her eventually move to the guest room.

His growing habit of staying overnight near the university before finally, a friend of my mother's had spotted him with the first of many young women.

Rubbing my forehead, I say, "I wanted to ask her Saturday. But I just... couldn't."

He hums in understanding. "I don't blame you, love."

"Don't call me that," I say tiredly.

"Iris..."

So much longing in the word.

I hang up.

———————

I spend Thanksgiving with Claire's family, who live north of Seattle in Everett. This isn't the first holiday meal I've crashed—more like the tenth—but her parents and kid brother love me.

In their cluttered, warm home, I find something I've always wanted and lacked: a cohesive, loving, and honest rapport. No family is perfect, of course, and I've witnessed enough petty fights to know the McHenry's aren't the Cleavers, but at the end of the day, they *belong* to each other. They're a real family.

Before dinner, as I'm helping pour gravy into boats, Claire's mom, Marsha, asks why I didn't fly home. The only response I can think of is, "Too much work with finals approaching."

It's not really true, as I haven't been doing anything *besides* schoolwork, but I'm sane enough to know the truth is a little too muddled for polite conversation.

"You need to stop working so hard," says Griffen amiably. "It's making the rest of us look bad."

I smirk. "I'm coming for you, 4.0."

He chuckles. "I should have volunteered to have Beckett be my proofreader on the first day of class."

I nod, my smile edging toward brittle. "It's a blessing and a curse, really. He shreds everything I give him to pieces, but my skin's thicker now." I shrug. "He's made me a better writer, so it's been worth it."

As Marsha leaves the room with a bowl of salad, Griffen clears his throat. "Are you... doing okay with that? Working with him?"

I shrug. "It's a little weird, but since we got back from the funeral he's been the consummate professional. And no offense, but I think he grades me harder than anyone."

Griffen nods, smiling brightly. "Oh, I know. You're the best writer of the bunch, and everything you turn in comes back with way more red scribbles than anyone else's. Now that I think of it, I take back my earlier statement. I'm really glad he's not my proofreader."

A knot of tension I wasn't aware of unravels at his words. "Thanks for noticing and for the complement, but I don't think it's true. You're an exceptional writer."

Claire enters the room from the dining room. "Sounds like a love fest in here. I like it." She wraps her arms around Griffen's waist. "Dinner's ready, kids. Oh, and be prepared for Jeremy to rant about animal cruelty while dad carves the turkey. Vegetarianism is his new thing. Just smile and nod."

Laughing, I grab my glass of champagne and follow them to the dining room.

Jeremy's spiel is as entertaining as expected, especially when he finds out that Griffen was raised on a functioning farm, complete with slaughterhouse. Although sixteen-year-old Jeremy probably has no clue, the rest of us can't help noticing the admiring gleam in his eye as Griffen shares about farm life.

Later, Claire and I make a wager on how long the vegetarianism will last. She bets one more day. I have a little more faith in Jeremy's idealism and bet a week.

After dessert of apple crumble, homemade ice-cream, and delicious french-pressed coffee, Griffen drives me back to the city.

When he pulls up to my apartment building, I jokingly ask, "You going to be okay without Claire this weekend?"

"I'm going to miss her a lot," he answers seriously. "It's our first weekend apart since we got together. But honestly I'm more worried about you. Are *you* going to be okay?"

"Touché," I say with a smile. "I think I'll live. Mainly because Claire stocked the fridge for me yesterday."

He laughs. "That doesn't surprise me. Well, if you need a ride anywhere, give me a call. I'll be writing all weekend."

"Will do." I open the door, then grin at him. "Just so you now, I'm godmother to your first baby."

To my surprise, he blushes. "I'll always owe you a debt of gratitude for introducing us. She's incredible."

I nod. "She is. Goodnight, Griff. Thanks for the ride."

"Sure thing."

I step into the cold and hustle into my building. In my apartment, I flip on lights and quickly adjust the heater to Human Living Here. As I'm taking off my coat, my phone buzzes. I grab my purse off the couch and rummage inside until I find it.

The alert is a three-word text from James.

Check your email

It's the first time he's contacted me outside of school in two weeks, and I can't help the nervous flutter in my belly. My thumb shakes a little as I open email on my device and see an unread message from j.s.beck. The subject line is *Eliot—final draft,* and the body of the message is empty.

I don't bother opening the attachment on my phone, but run to my room and power up my laptop. Pulling up my email, I download the attached file, then open it in my word processor. There's no title page, just a dedication. I run the tip of my finger across the words:

For Derrick and Iris Eliot

"Prick," I whisper through a smile.

Kicking off my shoes, I curl my legs beneath me and settle the laptop on my thighs. Over the next hours, my reading pauses only once, and then only because I'm crying so hard I can't see.

In his witty, crisp, elegant way, James has given me an unlocked portal to the heart and mind of a father I never really knew. The tale is grave and also beautiful. Joyful, yet ultimately heartbreaking. And when it's finished, I stare at the final sentences until they blur.

In the words of the poet himself, "The greatest among us step most softly; but oh, so mighty are their steps." For all his rich humanness, his pride and passion,

*Richard Eliot was without a doubt mighty. His foot-
steps, light as they were, left chasms in their wake.*

As I reach for my phone, I don't care that it's two o'clock in the morning. I know he's waiting. And he is.

"So?" he asks lightly, though I hear the thread of nervousness.

"Thank you," I whisper.

He sighs heavily. "You're welcome, of course. Iris—"

"I want the letters," I blurt.

"Of course. They're yours. Do you want me to bring them? This weekend? Or, wait, are you here or in California? I could send them. Wherever you want."

His uncharacteristic babbling makes me smile. "I'm here. Maybe you can bring them by tomorrow?"

"Yes, absolutely."

I take a deep breath. "James?"

"Yes?" he asks mutedly.

"It's missing something."

"I decided that story isn't mine to tell."

Thinking he's misunderstanding me, I say, "I'm not talking about what happened between my parents."

There was no mention of my mother's alleged affair, and I know that despite her initial agreement, she's since refused to speak with him about my father.

"I know, love," he murmurs. "I won't tell your story because it's yours. And you're writing it, aren't you?"

Goosebumps lift across my body. "How do you—"

"I saw you in the student union on Monday."

My mouth snaps closed so hard my teeth clack. I had lunch on Monday with Dr. Lisa Thompson, the faculty director of SARVA—Sexual Assault and Relationship Violence Activists—to find out more about the organization. And to gain a better understanding of the emotional Pandora's box that sits half-opened in my gut.

With roundabout questioning—a tactic I doubt was lost on Dr. Thompson—I'd discovered that blocking of sexual assault for months or even years isn't uncommon. Nor are the vivid punches of emotion that have been battering me for the last two weeks: shame, unfocused fear, white-hot anger.

Though the memories of the assault itself are still hazy, the emotional echoes slap me at the oddest times. While showering. Doing laundry. Brushing my teeth.

In order to manage them, to not fall apart and stay in bed for the next decade, I've been utilizing the only coping mechanism I have.

Writing.

A little breathlessly, I tell James, "You're a stalker."

"To the ends of the earth, my little muse."

My heart trips, then gallops. "I haven't forgiven you."

"Yes, you have. You just haven't admitted it to yourself yet."

A laugh bursts out of me. "You—you're—"

"A prick," he says lightly. "Do you have a draft yet?"

Dragging a hand down my flushed face, I reply, "Rough, yes."

"Let me read it."

"No!"

"Let me pitch it to my agent?"

"No!"

He chuckles. "I don't actually need your permission."

My breath goes choppy; panic closes around my chest. "James, I can't do this," I speak in a rush, hardly aware of my words. "I can't be yours. I can't. I don't know what we had, but it's over. You need to move on."

"You don't mean that," he says softly, the words so full of pain that my stomach clenches. I grip the phone so hard a knuckle pops.

"I do mean it."

And then I do something really stupid. Because I don't know how else to protect myself. How to manage the tumult in my heart, the damage of the past, and the shadowy unknown of the future. I lie through my teeth.

"I'm seeing someone. We have our third date this weekend. I like him a lot."

The words are clear, flawless. Even I can't tell that I'm a lying sack of shit.

His laughter is harsh in my ear. "Who?"

"You don't know him. I met him in the city."

There's a beat of silence. "You're fucking serious." Low, pained laughter. "Unbelievable. Just like that, you're throwing us away. Why?"

You're too much. Too confusing. I'm too afraid.

A silent sob seizes my chest. I choke it down and tell him part of the truth—or at least a truthful confession of my deepest fear.

"Whatever you feel for me, James, it's not real. I think you had a fantasy of me in your head from my father, from the letters... You see what you want to see, a makeshift person. A broken girl you want to save."

He groans past another low laugh. "You know what, Iris? Fine. You're right. My obsession with you has run its course, anyway. I'm exhausted from trying to build something on quicksand. Take care of yourself."

The line goes dead.

The sob claws free.

Part II

THREE YEARS LATER

20. exegesis

Falling back onto a too-soft mattress, I stretch my arms over my head and hear my back crack with released pressure. Then I roll my head wearily toward the other bed in the room, occupied by a redheaded woman in pajamas.

"If I don't see another hotel room for as long as I live, that won't be long enough."

Kim Collins, my PA, laughs as she flips through channels on the television. "At least this one has clean sheets. Remember Houston? Oh, look, it's a rerun of your Helen interview! Aww, you were so nervous that day but you did great. Your makeup was so flawless."

I grab a pillow and cover my face with it. How she has the energy to talk, much less with such verve, is a mystery to me. We just spent four hours at a signing.

The only thing I want more than sleep right now is silence.

"Oh, oh, this is my favorite part!" squeals Kim.

The volume increases until I can hear clearly despite my pillow buffer.

"SO, IRIS, THERE'S BEEN A LOT OF SPECULATION ABOUT COLE..." The audience screams and applauds. "OBVIOUSLY SINCE YOUR BOOK IS A MEMOIR, HE'S BASED ON A REAL GUY. HOW REAL ARE WE TALKING?" Laughter rises and fades.

"REAL ENOUGH, HELEN."

"UH OH, TEAM, SHE'S PLAYING HARDBALL."

More laughter, including mine. I sound perfectly amused and unoffended, but I remember the discomfort behind my fake smile. Thankfully, I've fielded questions about Cole enough times that I have an automatic answer.

"I'LL SAY THIS MUCH—YES, COLE WAS/IS A REAL PERSON WHO MADE A LASTING IMPACT ON MY LIFE. I CAN TRULY SAY THAT WITHOUT HIS GUIDANCE, I WOULD HAVE NEVER HAD THE COURAGE TO WRITE MY STORY."

"AND WHAT A STORY IT IS! LET'S ALL THANK IRIS FOR BEING HERE TODAY AND SPEAKING SO OPENLY WITH US ABOUT THE TOUGH TOPICS ADDRESSED IN HER BEST-SELLING MEMOIR, A POET'S DAUGHTER. IF YOU

HAVEN'T ALREADY READ IT—"

Kim changes the channel, yawning loudly. "Iris, you still awake?"

I don't say anything, my face safely concealed by my pillow. A minute later, the television shuts off and Kim settles into bed. With a click from her bedside lamp, the room darkens.

Alone with my thoughts, I think of the person the world knows as Cole Laughlin, a thirty-something businessman with whom I'd had a brief affair during graduate school. Blond. Brown eyes. Born and raised in Seattle. Owns a cat named Charlie.

Though I obviously made use of artistic license to conceal his identity, everything else was true to form. His wit, his mind, his passion.

James.

We catch an early morning flight out of Boston home to Seattle. Kim sleeps the entire way and though I'm exhausted, I've never harnessed the skill of relaxing on planes. Instead of soothing, the dull roar gives me a headache. Or maybe it's the recycled air, or a mild case of claustrophobia.

Whatever it is, I spend the flight daydreaming about

waking up in my own bed in my own house, a little two-bedroom cottage in Capitol Hill. I purchased it last year using the advance from my publisher as a downpayment.

Though I could have easily drawn on my father's inheritance to buy the place outright, the idea had been quickly discarded. I'd wanted to fail or succeed without his help.

Thankfully, the largest gamble of my life paid off. Shortly after publication, *The Poet's Daughter* hit top-ten lists around the world and lingered in the literary stratosphere for weeks on end.

Wanted or not, at least part of my success is due to my father's lasting celebrity, while another is owed to the relentless support of another, no less famous man.

Beginning with subtle plugs in routine interviews and social media, and ending with a popular article in the New Yorker, James Beckett almost singlehandedly launched my career. Within weeks of his article, I was flooded with requests for interviews. Radio, television, print. Speaking engagements, expanded book tours, panels...

The road to humility hasn't been easy, but nowadays I'm more thankful than resentful.

In the last year, I've spent a total of thirty-six weeks on the road. Now I'm finally on my way home for the foreseeable future. I can rest. Recoup. See my family.

Get to work writing the next Great American Novel, as my agent is fond of labeling the unwritten masterpiece.

No pressure.

With the time change, it's not quite eleven o'clock when we land. Kim, bright-eyed from her nap, hustles to the baggage claim with me trailing behind. Her suitcase is one of the first to appear.

She gives me a tight hug. "Call me in the next few days to check in, okay? Oh, and don't forget, next weekend you have that event on campus."

I'd completely forgotten. Blacked it out, probably. Nodding like it's all I've been thinking about, I assure her I'll look over the details. After another hug, she races outside to find her ride—her longterm boyfriend, Vic, who she hasn't seen in a month.

I face the conveyer belt just in time to see my bag moving beyond reach. Too frazzled and tired to race after it, I cross my arms to wait for it to come back around.

"Come here often, darlin'?" asks a low voice to my left.

Without looking at the man beside me, I elbow him in the ribs. Griffen yelps, then drops a heavy arm on my shoulders and squeezes me.

"Get off me, oaf," I say, grinning. "Your arm weighs more than I do."

He chuckles. "Ain't that the truth. That's your bag, right, with the red tag?" He points and I nod. Chivalry isn't dead, because without me having to ask, he darts forward and hauls my heavy suitcase off the carousel.

"My hero," I say, batting my eyelashes.

Griffen chuckles. "Come on, short-stuff. Claire's probably sweating bullets by now. She's parked in loading-only and you know she has that phobia of getting arrested by airport police."

Laughing, I follow him outside. Sure enough, as we approach Griffen's car I spot Claire in the driver's seat, her hands bouncing nervously on the steering wheel. When she sees us, she jumps out and races around the hood.

I think she might be more relieved to have an excuse to park than she is glad to see me, and mutter as much to Griffen. He laughs and rolls my suitcase to the trunk.

Claire gives me a bone-cracking hug. "I'm so glad you're home," she says, leaning back to reveal teary eyes.

She's been emotional for the last few weeks, ever since she and Griffen finalized their upcoming move to Houston. After spending the last three years working to save money, they're ready for the next chapter in their lives. Griffen's will start on his much-anticipated PhD, while Claire plans to pursue licensing as a Marriage and Family Therapist.

They're leaving right after Christmas, which is one of the main reasons I'm taking the rest of the year off.

After next weekend, that is.

The sky chooses that moment to unleash it's stormy promise. In the time it takes us to scramble into the car, the freezing rain drenches our uncovered heads. Laughing and sputtering, we wiggle out of our wet coats.

Griffen catches my gaze in the rearview mirror and grins. "Welcome home gift from the city."

I smile. "Thanks, Seattle." I buckle my seatbelt, sighing in contentment as Griffen maneuvers us out of the loading zone toward the airport's exit.

As we merge onto the freeway, Claire's hand extends back from the passenger seat, a folded piece of paper in her fingers.

"What's this?" I ask, taking it.

"Just something I saw in a bookstore yesterday. Thought you might want to know."

I open the single sheet.

BLUEBIRD BOOKS

IS PROUD TO PRESENT

AN EVENING WITH JAMES S. BECKETT

THURSDAY, DECEMBER 6TH

7 - 9 P.M.

LIMITED SEATING

FIRST COME FIRST SERVE

The event is tonight.

I stare at the words until they blur, then calmly fold the flyer and tuck it under my thigh. Gazing out the window, I watch rain making rivers on the glass and the moving scenery beyond.

Claire clears her throat. "Griffen and I are going. Wanna tag along?"

"I'll think about it."

Fully aware of what my answer means, she sighs and turns on the radio.

21. form

_P_art of the dilemma, as I see it, is that Bluebird Books is three blocks from my house. It also happens to be one of my favorite places to spend an afternoon. Or evening, as the case may be.

But that's not what makes me jump in the shower after a restless few hours of sleep. It doesn't guide my hands as I blow-dry my hair into loose waves, apply eyeliner and mascara to make my dark eyes pop, and paint the barest hint of rose on my lips. And it's not why I change my clothes several times before deciding on dark jeans and a dove-grey sweater that Claire once told me makes my skin glow.

The real problem is that I can't help myself. It's been over two years since I've seen him face to face. Two years is a long time. I'm not the same woman I was then, and I'm definitely not the same woman who, three years ago, so carelessly threw him away.

"You can do this," I tell my reflection. "You are a mature, confident woman and a bestselling author. Be kind and polite. Don't do anything stupid. He doesn't hate you. You'll be fine."

Chin up, Buttercup.

Heart pounding, I pull on rain boots and grab my scarf and coat. Wallet. Phone. House key. Lastly, I tuck my hardcover copy of my father's biography safely beneath my coat.

Outside, I'm relieved to find the rain on pause for my walk, and further gratified when despite the low temp, my knee barely twinges. My joy at being home is so great, I'm not even bothered when my carefully styled waves fall prey to the moist air and wind.

By the time the glowing facade of Bluebird Books appears, I'm feeling every inch as confident as I hoped to. I hang onto that confidence by the skin of my teeth as I duck inside and join the growing crowd. The central space of the bookstore has been cleared to make space for forty or so occupied folding chairs.

"Iris!"

My gaze snaps in the direction of Claire's voice. She and Griffen are grinning and waving from the front row.

I watch with dawning horror as Claire points to the seat beside hers.

An empty seat.

For me.

In the front row.

Chin up.

As I skirt around the crowd, I hear my name several times, but I'm too focused on trying not to trip to acknowledge anyone with more than distracted smiles. At the front, I cross the empty space between a single, vacant armchair and a table set up with a variety of hardcovers, including his most recent thriller that was released several months ago.

I barely make it to the seat beside Claire before my knees buckle.

She puts her head on my shoulder. "You look amazing. I knew you'd come. He'll be so glad to see you. You're my hero. Have I told you how gorgeous you look? That sweater is the perfect color—"

"Okay, okay," I say, laughing in spite of my nervousness. "I'm here. You won, my manipulative little fiend. I mean friend."

She giggles and checks her watch. "He's late."

Griffen leans forward to give me a meaningful look. "Why am I not surprised?"

I laugh, shaking my head. "If I had a dollar for every time Beckett was late to class—"

The rest of my sentence is lost in sudden applause. I turn forward just as James emerges from adjacent stacks and crosses to the armchair with a little wave. His denim-clad legs pass not three feet from mine. Over an untucked dress shirt, he's wearing a hunter green sweater that I know makes his eyes electric—if I had the nerve to look at his face.

Instead, I stare at his scuffed brown boots as he sits. Watch his hands as he uncaps a bottled water sitting on the small table beside his chair.

The feverish applause continues. It occurs to me that I'm not clapping, but I can't seem to make my arms move. Only when Claire elbows me do I snap out of it and bring my numb hands together.

"Alright, that's enough," comes his humored, achingly familiar voice.

Someone whistles loudly and James laughs. The sound pours into my ears and down my body, lifting goosebumps. I'm seconds from bolting when Claire's hand clamps on my bouncing knee.

Eventually the applause fades. A bookstore employee walks into the space before James' chair.

"On behalf of Bluebird Books, I want to thank

everyone for this incredible turnout. Consider your-selves the lucky ones—we're at capacity and no one else is getting in!" She waits for a round of cheers to subside before speaking again.

"As you all know, tonight our guest is the legendary James Beckett. Acclaimed poet, novelist, and Director of the Creative Writing program at our very own U-Dub. The agenda this evening is flexible as per the author's request. He'll do a brief reading from *Indigo,* his newest thriller, then we'll, uh..."

James leans forward. "See how the night goes."

Laughter from the crowd.

Terrified and hopeful, I will my gaze to his face. But he's not looking at me, instead busying himself with several hardcovers on the display table. I take the time to absorb his features, to catalogue the evidence of years.

His hair is shorter on the sides but still a mess on top. He's clean shaven. Elegant and piratical. Exactly as I remember him, as though no time at all has passed.

Releasing a breath, I slump back in my chair.

"Looks the same, huh?" whispers Claire, and I nod.

The bookstore employee disappears and slowly, quiet descends on the gathering. James settles back in the chair, idly flipping pages until he finds the passage he wants. Bookmarking it with a finger, he looks up.

I look down.

"Thanks for coming, although I'm guessing most of you are my students. For your information, attendance this evening will not be counted as extra credit, a concept I firmly believe should be abolished from all centers of higher learning."

As laughter and groans sound, I glance around me. Sure enough, most people in the crowd are in their early twenties, faces bright and fresh.

"And what's this? Do my eyes deceive me?"

Light, teasing tone. I wonder if anyone else can hear the undercurrent of true surprise.

My gaze snaps to him. To startled green eyes aimed directly at me. My heartbeat thunders, breathing going shallow. I give him shaky smile, unable to look away, unable to keep the emotion from my face.

God, I've missed you.

James clears his throat and breaks eye contact. "Friends, we have among us a legend in her own right." A graceful hand extends toward me. "Iris Eliot, everyone."

I don't hear the applause, don't feel Claire's shoulder nudging mine. All I see is the casual affection that was in his eyes when he looked at me. Not desire. Not need. Just the look of someone staring at the past with no ill feelings. Someone who's made peace and moved on.

I lift my hand in a little wave to the appreciative crowd. Force a smile onto my face. Grip the hardcover in my lap like it's a life preserver.

All while my heart pounds, and withers, and turns to ash.

22. genre

"On her hip was a scar. Old and faded, smooth like a pebble worn by water, and so close to her healthy skin tone that I didn't at first notice it. It wasn't until she shifted onto her side that firelight danced there, teasing a sheen from the spot.

"I traced the small line with my fingertip, feeling her body tense, then relax. I wouldn't ask where it came from. She would tell me in time. For now, the gift of her brave nakedness was enough.

"My touch, though lingering, only skimmed the surface of her dreams. She lay still and hard and smooth before me, a chrysalises awaiting transformation. Soon, she would break free, and I would revel in witnessing her metamorphosis."

*J*ames closes the book, setting it on the small table with his water as the crowd applauds. He's just finished the third and final passage from *Indigo*. I haven't read it, and now I'm not sure I want to.

Did he read that on purpose?

Of course he did.

But I don't know whether it was meant to wound or heal. Perhaps both.

"All right, then," he says gravely. "I'm yours for the next hour and a half. Ask whatever you want, but do try to be original."

Hands shoot up all around the room.

"You there, red shirt."

"Hi, Mr. Beckett. Who's your favorite author?"

I wince; it's a question writer's loathe. Once you reveal your most-admired peers, oftentimes your works are weighed against theirs for the length of your career.

"Myself, of course."

Clever man, I acknowledge privately as the crowd laughs.

"How about you with the red lips. I'm indulging in a theme, clearly."

A young female voice asks, "Hi, professor. I'm

wondering if you'll ever publish another book of poetry?"

"Fancy you should ask. There's one in the works as we speak. It's slated for release next year. Ah, how about you with the questionable piercing in your nose. You've got a red scarf, at least."

The man laughs. "Thanks. Do you get your inspiration from people or events in your life, or do you just think it all up?"

"All of the above," replies James. "You might find yourself in one of my books one day. I'm not likely to forget that ornament on your face anytime soon. Ah, Griffen Banks, it's good to see you. Question?"

"Is it true that you almost didn't publish *Footprints of a Poet,* the biography on Richard Eliot?"

I stiffen, looking up to see James' smother a frown. He clears his throat. "It's true that my publisher wasn't happy with certain elements of the book, yes. But I'm a stubborn bloke, and they eventually came around."

Before James can pick someone else, Griffen asks a followup question. "Why weren't they happy with it?"

Green eyes flicker to me. "Writing biographies is tricky business, and sometimes the truth isn't black and white."

When he calls for the next question, I release the

breath I'd been holding. Leaning toward Claire, I hiss, "What the fuck was that?"

She looks at me guiltily. "Just something we thought you should know."

"God save me from meddling friends," I whisper back.

She winks.

"Ms. Eliot," says a carrying voice, "am I boring you?"

Claire squeaks in surprise, while Griffen barks a laugh. By some miracle of inner fortitude, I don't blush as I meet James' laughing eyes.

"I'm just waiting for the juicy stuff."

The crowd titters; someone whistles.

Lips twitching, James leans forward to brace elbows on his knees. A lock of hair falls across his forehead, begging me to brush it away.

"Like what?" he asks.

I'm spared a fumbling response when a woman shouts from the back: "Is it true you're getting married again?"

In the resulting cacophony, I feel the blood drain from my head. The smoldering ashes in my chest flare, then darken.

"Are you offering to be my bride?" asks James, skillfully dodging the question.

More whistles. Several yelled proposals and a few

brazen propositions. And an empty cavity where my heart used to be.

———

If not for Claire's ironclad grip on my hand, I would have run out the second the event was over. Instead, I find myself in line to get an autograph I don't want.

Unable to escape without embarrassing myself, I decide I'll donate the book. I've already read it six times, and I can always buy another copy.

When it's my turn, James doesn't look up, merely opening the cover and asking who he should make it out to.

"Just a signature is fine, thanks."

His head whips up, his gaze piercing as he catalogues my features with the same concentration as the first time we met. Only now he, too, is marking time. I don't know what he sees, but whatever it is brings a softness to his expression.

"It's lovely to see you, Iris."

"You, too." I shift nervously, aware of the line pressing at my back. "Really, just an autograph is fine."

He watches me a moment longer, then nods and bends to the book. When he offers it back to me, our fingers touch. Need and helplessness spike through me. The words *I miss you* bead on my lips. His eyes meet mine, questioning and a little guarded.

"Thanks," I choke out, and drag Claire away from the table.

"That was awkward," she mutters.

"No thanks to you," I mutter back.

We find Griffen waiting near the front door, where he helps Claire into her coat. "Do you want to come grab some late dinner with us, short-stuff?"

I shake my head. "Thanks, but I'm going home to bed. Jetlagged."

Claire kisses my cheek. "I'm proud of you. You're the bravest woman I know."

I muster a laugh. *The gift of her brave nakedness...* The words sweep through my mind, igniting memory and loss. Blinking hard against a sting in my eyes, I tell my friends goodnight and watch them walk outside.

With a pause to tuck my book under my coat, I follow. The temperature has dropped further and within ten feet, my knee begins to ache. A block later, I'm limping.

Gritting my teeth, I push forward. Just like I've always done. *Keep swinging.* I arm myself with thoughts of my warm house, ibuprofen, a hot bath, and my bed.

One foot in front of the other.

"Iris, wait!"

I stop too fast and almost trip, catching myself at the last second on a mailbox. By the time I turn around, James is standing before me.

"Jesus," he pants, "I thought you were going to fall."

The new, older, more experienced me says, "I don't need you to catch me anymore, James."

He frowns. "Let me walk you home."

"No, thank you."

"Iris—"

"Really, I'm fine."

Silence descends and stretches. He begins to shiver in his sweater.

I wave a hand in the direction of the bookstore. "You're not done signing, Mr. Famous."

His eyes find mine. "That's it, then? We're strangers?"

Words clash on my tongue, intelligible and base. *No. Home. Want you. Miss you. I'm sorry. So, so sorry. Are you really engaged? Please say no.*

After another pregnant silence, he sighs, breath descending in a misty cloud.

"We can't be friends, can we?" he asks softly.

I swallow hard. "I don't think so."

A final time, his gaze flies over my face. "Goodbye, Iris."

I watch him walk away until his figure turns a corner, then reach under my coat for the book he signed. Opening it in the light of a nearby streetlamp, I read his slanted handwriting.

Little Muse,
I am, as always, your servant.
J.S.B.

Astoundingly, I make it home before falling apart.

23. hubris

After bawling my eyes out and sleeping eleven hours straight, I wake up with newfound conviction.

It's time to let go of James Beckett.

Easier said than done, of course, but I begin the process by retrieving a shoebox from the attic. Inside are the letters I wrote him and never sent, as well as the stack of letters from my father. The latter, I put back in the box.

I spend the morning reading with a box of tissues handy. When I finish, I throw them in the trash. Ten minutes later I retrieve them. Then I trash them again. After repeating the cycle another few times, I finally call Claire. She comes over, listens to me rant and rave, and grabs the letters from the trashcan.

"Hell no are these getting dumped. You're famous. I might need them someday."

She stuffs them in her purse, fierce expression daring me to object. I don't. I'm just relieved to have them gone.

The bulk of the next few days are spent doing home-owner-ey things like stocking my pantry and fridge, mopping the floors, doing laundry, and decorating walls with various paintings and photos that I never found time to hang.

By Saturday afternoon, I'm restless. I have plans to meet Claire and Griffen for dinner this evening, but I can't spend one more hour pretending I'm too busy cleaning to write.

Hoping for inspiration, I pack a thermos of coffee and my journal and pens and head to Bluebird Books. Inside the warm, bustling store, the tables and furniture are back where they normally are. No traces of Thursday's event remain save the display table devoted to Beckett's works.

In one of the side rooms, I'm lucky enough to spy an empty armchair. The alcove holds two, and in the other sits a student with headphones on and a laptop on their knees, a stack of reference books at their feet. *Perfect.*

I take off my coat and toe out of my rain boots, then sit crosslegged in the chair. Diluted sunshine floats through the window at my back, wreathing my shoulders. With a sigh, I settle back and close my eyes.

Fingers on paper. Dust and ink. Whispered voices, a few louder ones. The muted *ting ting* of a cash register. Clacking of computer keys as the student writes.

The sounds and scents are a writer's lullaby, coaxing me to sleep.

"**B**ook tours are exhausting, aren't they?"

My eyes snap open at the familiar voice. Mind muddled by the unexpected nap, I lift my head and look around blearily. The window behind me shows a dark sky, and the student has been replaced by sexy, British man.

"Hello, Iris."

"Shit," I reply, sitting up and rubbing my face roughly.

His lips tilt sardonically. "I've been called worse things, I'm sure."

Still struggling for clarity, I blurt, "Am I dreaming?"

"Do you dream of me often?"

This time, there's no controlling my blush. "No," I lie, scowling. "How long have you been sitting there?"

"Long enough to become reacquainted with your snoring."

My mouth drops. "I don't snore!"

He winks. "Don't worry, I won't tell a soul."

Groaning, I rummage in my coat for my cell phone. It isn't there, so I grab my messenger bag from the floor.

"What time is it? What are you even doing here?"

"Late for a date? And I'll have you know I'm a frequent visitor here." He holds up a familiar black journal, then nods to the one still in my lap. "I think we had the same idea."

My fingers close on my phone. I check the time and curse, then send Claire a text to let her know I'm going to be late to dinner.

"A date?" asks James.

"I heard you the first time, and like the first time, I'm ignoring you."

Chuckling, he watches me stuff my journal into my bag. When I stand, he stands with me. We're close enough that I can smell his cologne, which triggers a powerful wave of sensory memory.

My heart dusts itself off and kicks hard. Lifting my chin, I force myself to meet his eyes.

"Don't you have a girlfriend to get home to?"

His smile turns sharp. "We don't live together."

I smother a flinch. "Well, either way, you need to stop looking at me like that."

"Like what?"

I wave a hand in his direction. "You know, like *that*."

He takes a step forward, his eyes never leaving mine. The warmth of his body radiates onto my skin. I'm frozen in place as he bends his head to whisper in my ear.

"I'm still a prick, little muse. And I still want to fuck you silly."

I reel backward, both in surprise and shameful arousal. James grabs the lapels of my coat before I tumble into a cabinet full of books.

"And besides," he says lightly, "Jessica and I have an agreement."

"An agreement?" I echo. "What the hell does that mean?"

He shrugs a shoulder. "We're not exclusive. And definitely not getting married."

Slowly, anger outshines my desire. "Are you serious right now? You're propositioning me while in a relationship with another woman?"

"An *open* relationship," he corrects. "And yes, I suppose I am. You're even more stunning than I remember. I'd be an idiot not to at least make an attempt."

Disgusted and no longer the least bit aroused, I yank

away from him. "Who are you and what have you done with James?"

He smiles but it's distant and cool, not reflecting in his eyes. "I'm a pragmatist, pet. And perhaps a bit of a masochist. You handed me my bleeding heart on a platter three years ago. I'm not offering it to you again. But I have very fond, very vivid memories of that sweet, tight little body."

"Stop! Just stop. Is this revenge? A way to get back at me for a stupid lie I told out of fear?"

James blinks in surprise; belatedly, I realize my error.

"You lied," he growls. "You weren't seeing anyone."

With a soft cry of frustration, I snap, "Of course not. With everything I was dealing with at the time, did you really think I'd found some random guy to date? My delayed PTSD from the night of the accident was so bad I barely left my apartment."

Agonized, angry green eyes find mine.

"Damn you, Iris."

He brushes past me and disappears around a corner. I hear the bell of the front door, and moments later see him stalk past the window, head uncovered and bent into the light rain.

He was right—the truth isn't always black and white. But whatever color it manifests as, sometimes it just hurts.

24. hyperbole

_M_y first reading and signing on campus was shortly after _A Poet's Daughter_ was released. It was held in a classroom with all of thirty people in attendance, most of them friends and former teachers. James hadn't shown, but I couldn't blame him. By that time we hadn't spoken in close to a year, not since my graduation ceremony.

This event is different on all counts.

The lecture hall is massive and filled wall to wall. A giant video camera is set up to record the evening, and sitting in the front row are top university benefactors and faculty. The audience is also not limited to students and teachers, but filled with people of all ages and walks of life.

And seated beside me onstage is James, waiting for the go-ahead to introduce me at the nearby lectern.

He's barely looked at me since I arrived. As the silent, tense minutes tick by, I feel so alone, so lost and anxious, that I find myself reaching out to the girl I was when I fell in love with him.

"I think I'm going to puke."

James finally looks at me, brows raised. "You've done events like this, haven't you?"

"Yes, but not on my home turf, and not with you sitting next to me projecting enough animosity to frizz my hair."

His lips quirk, humor softening the severe green of his eyes. "Your hair is perfect," he murmurs, "but you really need to stop fidgeting."

I clench my hands in my lap and press down to halt the nervous tapping of my foot. The stillness only magnifies the sour rolling of my stomach.

"Distract me," I whisper pleadingly.

His eyes narrow. "I'm not sure I want to."

"Please, James."

He sighs, sprawling back in his chair with his legs crossed at the ankles. He didn't bother to dress up for the event, opting to wear a casual sweater, worn jeans, and his favorite scuffed boots. If he wasn't so famous and didn't bring such renown to the university, he'd be fired for being a disrespectful slob.

"Distracted you," he says with a wink.

My cheeks go hot. "You couldn't bother with a suit?"

His eyes drag across my mouth. "Now why would I do that when you love me dressed down?"

Swallowing, I look away. One of the event organizers catches my eye from beside the video camera and holds up five fingers.

Five minutes.

I hope I last that long.

"Tell me a story," I beg James.

"Hmm, let me think." He pauses. "All right, here you go. Once upon a time, there was a young woodland nymph with the face of an angel but the eyes of a devil, so dark that to look into them was to see the unplumbed depths of one's own soul. There was pain in those eyes, and loneliness, but in her long, immortal life, she'd never met anyone who understood her pain and thus became a cold and calculating creature.

"Our nymph spent her days frolicking in the forests of her native Scotland and her nights dancing naked beneath the moon and mist. Ageless and beguiling, she trapped young men for sport, toying with them until she tired of them, then tossing them out of her glade with no memory of the time spent in her arms."

In my peripheral vision, I see the event coordinator hold up three fingers. I barely comprehend the gesture, all of me focused on the voice of the man beside me.

"Then one day, a strapping young man set out to find the nymph. He, unlike the others, didn't seek her for pleasure or to win a wager, but because he, too, was alone in his pain. He searched for months, growing ever more tired and ragged, before finally stumbling one evening into the nymph's glade. She looked at him and he at her, and they knew one another. At their first touch, the young man felt a peace unlike any he'd known before. He instantly fell madly and deeply in love.

"But alas, the nymph wasn't a human woman, and she didn't know how to give the man love in return. In time, she rejected him as she'd done all the others. Only when he was gone did she regret her choice and feel again the loneliness he had assuaged. To this day, she waits alone, dancing in the moonlight and mist, for a man long dead to return."

As the vibrations of his voice fade from my ears, the world rushes to the fill the vacuum. Hundreds of faces engaging in chatter and laughter and sneezes and coughs.

The coordinator holds up one finger and waves urgently at James, but he doesn't see her. He's watching me. Watching me blink back tears. Watching me struggle to get my breathing under control.

"Iris," he breathes.

"Mr. Beckett!" shouts the coordinator.

He finally looks away from me and sees the now-frantically waving woman. Without another word, he stands and approaches the lectern. I watch him visibly regain composure, his spine straightening while his overall posture relaxes.

"Good evening," he says in his usual cultured, faintly amused tone. "I had a fancy speech prepared but my dog ate it."

The audience laughs; I smile sadly, thinking of Rufus and how entirely feasible his statement is.

"So instead of blathering on about how proud I am of the woman sitting to my left, how many bestseller lists she's dominated, and how many stodgy critics she's romanced with her pen, I'll tell you something different. Something that we tend to regrettably forget in our worship of the Next Young Talent.

"I assume most of you have read *A Poet's Daughter*, but I wonder how many of you understand that the woman whose tale you so greedily consumed is real. Living and breathing despite all that has happened to her.

"Do you know that 33% of women who are victims

of assault have suicidal thoughts? That a startling 13% attempt suicide? Here's another one for you: one in six women in this country have been sexually assaulted." His eyes flow over the sea of faces. "I'd guess roughly two-thirds of you are women. This hall holds around seven hundred. That means nearly eighty women in this room have been victimized."

James pauses; the silence is deafening. I can hear the hum of voices in a neighboring hall. I can hear my own pounding heart.

"Do you know that Iris Eliot receives hate-mail blaming her for her own assault? I want you to think about that tonight. Think about the courage necessary to stand up here and be prodded, and criticized, and judged by your peers. Then imagine yourself in her shoes. I guarantee none of you can scratch the surface of this woman's bravery, intelligence, or depth with a question. I dare you to try."

He stands still for another moment, then looks my way.

"Ladies and gentlemen, let me present to you the unmatched Iris Eliot."

Somehow, I get my legs under me and stand. One step at a time, one breath at a time, I make it to the lectern.

The crowd is applauding, cheering, but all I see is

James. His white knuckles gripping the side of the podium. The erratic rise and fall of his chest. His eyes, vivid with the same emotion that colored his voice. Anger. Frustration. Appeal.

I think he's going to grab me. Kiss me in front of all these people. But he doesn't. He gives me a quick, impersonal peck on the cheek and strides past me to his chair.

My head spinning and body trembling, I face the microphone. The applause fades away.

"Thank you, Professor Beckett." I clear my throat. "Does anyone have any whiskey?"

James' laughter rings loudest in my ears.

25. imagery

When the final book is signed, the final hand shaken, and final platitudes exchanged, I walk wearily to the first row and sink into a padded seat. I stare at the shadowed stage and for the hundredth time, regret my odd quirk of always wanting to be the last to leave a signing.

Besides Kim, who's gathering our belongings, the videographer is the only one left in the now-cavernous space. As I watch, he finishes packing the tools of his trade, gives me a nod and wave, and departs.

Kim sinks down beside me, our purses at her feet. "Holy shit that was draining. I need a drink."

I smirk tiredly. "Preaching to the choir."

She fixes bloodshot blue eyes on my face. "How do

you do it, Iris? How do you stand up there and talk about that night over and over again?"

This isn't the first time she's asked me, but tonight's Q&A was especially difficult. An unintended side-effect of James' challenge was that every question was more probing and personal than the last.

I shrug, closing my tired eyes. "Honestly, speaking about it has been more cathartic than the writing was. Not that it ever becomes rote, but the repetition helps me see it for what it is—something that happened, not something that defines me."

She's silent for a few moments, mulling over my words. "Yeah, well, you're way more spiritually advanced than me. I almost killed that bitch who accused you of reinforcing rape culture because you never pressed charges."

I wince, remembering what happened right after the woman asked the—yes, blatantly accusatory—question.

Kim continues, "Although it was pretty awesome watching James Beckett go to town on her."

And he had, yanking the microphone away from my stunned face and scathingly educating the woman on evidence versus hearsay, statute of limitations, the emotional cost of a public trial, and the statistics of a favorable verdict.

"You know," Kim muses through a yawn, "you guys

looked super hot up there together. And he's not your professor anymore..."

I snort. "Been there done that."

Kim bolts upright and grabs my arm, enlivened by the possibility of gossip. I crack open an eye and chuckle at her rapt, open-mouthed expression.

"Oh my God, you've boned James Beckett? *The* James Beckett? Why did I not know this?"

I laugh again to cover the squeeze of pain in my chest. "It's water under the bridge."

"Is it, little muse?"

Kim gasps, I choke on breath, and we swivel in our chairs to see James sitting several rows behind us. In the dim lighting, his hair in disarray and his feet propped on the row before him, he looks even more rakish than usual.

More accustomed to his blinding sex appeal than Kim, I recover first. "You were eavesdropping, really? How old are you?"

He grins and I swear I can feel Kim swoon. A second later she's on her feet and grabbing her purse.

"I have to, um, go," she stammers, ruining the lie with a giggle.

Resigned, I watch her hasten from the hall. The heavy door squeals as it opens and clanks as it closes behind her.

James doesn't bother with the stairs at the end of the row, easily traversing the space between us by virtue of balance and long legs.

When he plops into Kim's recent seat, I drop my head back and once again close my eyes, this time to savor his presence. To allow myself to imagine a different past and a new future for us. But my fantasy is short-lived, collapsing under the weight of his fable's final words.

To this day, she waits alone, dancing in the moonlight and mist, for a man long dead to return. He couldn't have been more clear. The man I loved and threw away is gone.

Facing the emotional consequences of my actions, I square my shoulders and open my eyes. He's watching me, one brow quirked in question. Or challenge.

I clear my throat. "Though you didn't have to, thank you for coming to my defense tonight."

"You're welcome," he says, glancing at the shadowed lectern. "But you're right, I didn't have to. You would have wiped the floor with her all on your own."

"Maybe." A grin steals my lips. "But I wouldn't have done it so creatively. Imbecilic *minger*? I had to Google what that meant."

He chuckles. "Despite the inevitable reprimand in

my future, I don't regret it. And she *was* ugly, at least on the inside."

I nod, my smile fading as I take a deep breath and pray for the courage to speak the truth. "Thank you, James, for everything—your mentoring during my final year, for the beautiful biography of my father, for the support of my book..." My words trail off, squeezed back by fear.

For your belief in me.

For your belief in us.

For showing me that my scars are beautiful.

Green eyes spear mine; as always, I feel transparent beneath his gaze. "Like I told you from the beginning, your talent absolutely floors me. And in case that doubtful mind of yours ever wonders, falling for you had nothing to do with my academic or professional decisions."

I crack a smile. "I know. If anything, you graded me ten times harder than anyone else."

He swallows hard, gaze dropping to my lips. My breath catches and I sway toward him, my body over-taken by a powerful, unconscious drive to consume him and be consumed.

"James?" I whisper. "What are we doing?"

"No clue. As I said, I'm a masochist." He licks his

lips. "But if you keep looking at me like that, I might think you'll let me bend you over these chairs."

"Is this punishment for not bending over for you?"
"Interesting choice of words, Ms. Eliot, but with you I'd prefer face to face."

Our long-ago conversation ripples through my mind, confirming what I already know. It doesn't make the knowledge any less painful. Nor does it relieve the ache I feel when, for brief moments, the man I loved resurfaces.

A man long dead.

A man I slew with my cowardice.

A man I'm still too much of a coward to tell how I feel—that I loved him three years ago and still do, that I dream about Sunday breakfasts with him, rolling on the floor with Rufus, and rainy nights of chess and cuddling on the couch.

The lecture hall's doors open with a screech.

"James? Have you said your goodbyes yet? I'm starving!"

The petulant female voice resonates thanks to the lecture hall's acoustics. Sharp heels clack toward us. A woman appears at the mouth of the small corridor, highlighted by the recessed lighting above her. As I take her in, a knot of dread builds in my stomach.

She's a beautiful brunette, tall and willowy. Beneath her fashionable black trench coat is a tight emerald dress that accentuates her smooth, creamy skin and tiny waist. Her lips are carmine, her eyes boldly lined, and her features both sensuous and exotic.

James stands, waving her forward. She walks toward us, a wet dream on stilettos. When she's close enough, he gives her a soft kiss near her ear. And when they face me, they're holding hands.

"Jessica, meet Iris Eliot. Iris, this is Jessica Buchanan. She's an architect at a firm downtown."

I can't move. Can't speak. Can't summon even the barest modicum of civility. And neither can she, apparently.

"I haven't read your book but I'm sure it's interesting." She turns to James. "Can we go?"

My mouth falls open in shock. I look at James, expecting to see annoyance or hear his defense of me, but he merely shakes his head chidingly at Jessica. His smile is tolerant and amused, reminding me once again of the truth I haven't fully accepted.

He's not the same person.

Not mine.

"Of course, Jessica," he says, then smiles at me. His eyes are distant, unfamiliar. "Congratulations again on the impressive turnout tonight. Take care, Iris."

He slips an arm around Jessica's waist. She smiles coyly at me as they turn and walk toward the exit. They move gracefully, their bodies in tune, two tall and slim silhouettes.

Before they leave my line of sight, I see Jessica's hand skate down his broad back, tuck into a pocket of his jeans, and squeeze. I hear his soft, answering chuckle.

Dry-eyed and numb, I sit in the empty hall until an overnight janitor enters with a vacuum. Then I gather my purse from the floor and make the long, limping walk to my car.

By the time I arrive home, I've considered and discarded a hundred different plans for my future.

Moving to Canada.

Following Claire and Griffen to Houston.

Buying a farm in Santa Cruz.

Joining a commune, preferably overseas.

Pursuing my PhD at the University of Edinburgh, Scotland.

Although the last holds some appeal and is considered the longest, I eventually discard it, too. I've run away so many times in my life, a self-made victim of my emotions. I've run from my father, from memory, from pain, and out of fear, doubt, and self-loathing.

For a girl with a bum knee, I've been running a long time.

Maybe it's time to stop.

26. irony

I spend Christmas in Palo Alto. With a newfound conviction to be present and invested in my life, I finally claim the family that has been waiting for me for years.

Phillip, Victoria, and Allison are as overjoyed as always to have me, only this time I embrace the gift. I participate wholeheartedly in every silly tradition they have, and enjoy myself more than I ever imagined I would.

There's checkers and charades and peppermint hot chocolate on Christmas Eve, and on Christmas morning we stuff ourselves with peppermint pancakes and choco-late bacon (I had no idea that was a thing). After break-fast, we settle in the family room to open presents, which

Victoria distributes one at a time based on the alphabetical order of our first names.

The traditions continue in the afternoon with a completely insane amount of home-cooked food. Catatonic and happy, we spend the evening watching Christmas movie classics and sipping peppermint eggnog.

By the time my mom drives me to the airport the following day, I have plans for dinner with Allison when she gets back to Seattle, gifts crammed into every corner of my carry-on, and a vehement desire to never eat or drink anything flavored with peppermint again.

After securing a promise to visit in a few months, my mom shoos me off with tears in her eyes.

I smile the whole flight home.

Not until I let myself into my dark house does loneliness return. And oh, it returns with a vengeance. In lieu of impulsively adopting a pet, I counter the emptiness around me with the only outlet I have

I write. Page after page in journals and on my laptop. I have no idea what I'm writing about, or whether it will eventually take the shape of a novel. But I'm writing and that's enough.

It has to be enough.

New Year's Eve, Claire and Griffen pick me up at eight and we head downtown for dinner and drinks at our favorite Italian restaurant. Along with the multitude of happy couples around us and our empty fourth chair, we ignore the elephant in the room: they're leaving at the end of the week for Houston.

After delicious chicken cacciatore—and three stiff drinks—it's easier to forget that my best friends are moving away. Griffen is especially helpful in that department, as he's the most jolly drunk I've ever had the pleasure of drinking with. His accent also thickens, which amuses the sober Claire to no ends.

It's close to eleven by the time she manages to corral us into the car. Somehow, Griffen and I end up in the backseat together. As Claire drives us through the glittering night, he belts out his favorite country song, only he's drunk enough that he forgets most of the words.

Laughing so hard I'm crying, I don't notice where we're going until Claire parks in a tiny slot in a narrow alley.

"That sign says Reserved, Claire-bear," I say, leaning between the front seats.

She grins at me. "Tonight it's reserved for us."

Squinting, I can just make out the faded business name on the sign drilled into the brick wall. My eyes widen with recognition, then veer to her happy face.

"Oh my gosh, this is so perfect," I squeal. "I can't believe I didn't think of it."

White Harp Pub.

She laughs. "Our last hurrah in our school-days bar. I couldn't resist."

"White Harp?" Griffen hoots, finally catching up. "Aww, hunnybear, this is the best surprise ever."

"Hunnybear?" I hiss out of the corner of my mouth.

Claire just laughs and turns off the car. "We have VIP privileges tonight, kids. Clock's ticking—let's go!"

We grab our coats and emerge into the cold, crisp air. As Griffen swings Claire around and covers her face in sloppy kisses, I bang on the steel door with faded scroll-work and lettering. Moments later, it opens on the smiling face of the bar's longterm manager, Henry Leary.

He beams at us, arms spread wide. "My favorite customers! Right on time. Forty-five minutes till the new year!"

I give Henry's rotund middle a squeeze, then hustle past him into the warmth of the pub's back hallway. Music and voices flow over me along with a colorful cascade of memories.

Once Griffen and Claire wrap up their love-fest, Henry leads us to a roped-off booth with a *Reserved* card on it. It's the only vacant spot in the place. Removing the velvet rope with flourish, he gestures us forward. I can't stop grinning as he takes our drink order and heads to the bar.

Around the crowded space I spy many familiar faces, former students and faculty alike, and just as many unfamiliar ones. Pride and nostalgia mingle as the three of us end our long tenure and celebrate the newer generation of students staking their claim to the venerated pub.

Visitors to our table come and go over the next half-hour. In the interims, we trade our best memories of White Harp—and a few we'd rather forget.

"Remember that freshman you TA'd a class for?" Claire asks me, her eyes bright with mirth. I groan, knowing exactly who she's referring to.

"Mark? Mike?" I ask, wincing.

"We'll go with Mike." Struggling to contain laughter, she turns to Griffen. "He'd been crushing hard on her all quarter, leaving anonymous notes and flowers on her desk—the whole nine yards. The weekend after finals, Iris and I were here having a few drinks, decompressing and whatnot, when Mike showed up with some friends. He stared at Iris for a freaking *hour* before approaching her. I remember the look on her face so well—resignation and sympathy. She was going to let him down easy, but the poor kid didn't get one word out."

Griffen laughs. "What, he ran away?"

"Oh, no," says Claire, giggling wildly. "He opened his mouth and puked all over her."

Griffen chokes on his beer, spits a mouthful back into the glass, then laughs so hard his face turns red. Claire pats him on the back, laughing along with him.

I roll my eyes. "He ruined my favorite shirt."

From the bar comes Henry's megaphone-enhanced voice, "*Five minutes, people!*"

Claire squeals and straps a sparkly party hat on Griffen's head, then pulls on one of her own. When she reaches for me with another, I jump out of the booth.

"I'm going for a refill."

Griffen points behind me. "It's insanity right now! You'll be crushed!"

I glance at the sea of people between me and the bar, then shrug. "I'm wily. Plus, we're VIP, right? See you guys in a few."

I wave and turn away before I can see the compassion and gratitude in Claire's eyes. She knows the twofold reason I'm escaping. This was where their romance began, and I want to give them the magic of a private New Year's kiss. And I also don't want to be the awkward third party with no date.

So depressing.

I don't bother trying to reach the bar. Griff was right—there's no way I'm getting through without bruises. Skirting along the edge of the crowd, I head for the front. It takes some time and when I finally get there, the countdown is starting.

"10... 9... 8..."

I duck past a screaming celebrant and out the front door into relative peace and quiet. The sidewalks are virtually empty; a few stragglers hurry to stomp out ciga-rettes and join indoor celebrations. Further down the street, light and voices spill into the night from other bars.

I lean against the damp wall between White Harp and the dark bakery next door. Eyes closed, I smile as I listen to the distorted din of hundreds of voices counting.

"3... 2... 1!"

In the following roar, I don't notice the sound of a car door slamming and running footsteps. When hands grab my shoulders, I gasp, my eyes snapping open. But my momentary panic is decimated by a sucker punch of emotion to my heart.

"I knew I'd find you, little muse."

And then his mouth is on mine, hard and hot and

urgent. Familiar and not. I melt against him, opening for his tongue.

He tastes the same.

My James.

With a guttural groan, he lifts me and backs me into the wall. My legs instinctively circle his hips. We feed on each other, artless and animalistic, insatiable after such a long drought.

I wonder if I'm dreaming.

He grinds into me, hard and thick against the seam of my jeans. "Does this feel like a dream?"

"Yes," I gasp.

He nips my lower lip and draws back. Drugged by arousal, I slowly open my eyes. He's still there. Still holding me, his strong fingers under my thighs.

"James?" I ask, my voice small and hopeful.

He shakes his head. "No. Don't, please. Just... can we forget it all tonight? I need to be inside you." He rocks against me and I whimper. "That's all I want. Please."

I nod.

Knowing I'll regret it tomorrow, I still nod.

Because as much as he needs me, I need him more. And right now, I'll gladly take scraps from his table.

Once in James' warm car, I text Claire that I found a ride home and wish her and Griffen a Happy New Year. Then I give James my address before he can ask for it, or worse, suggest a hotel.

I know he doesn't want me in his house. Doesn't want me to see Rufus. Doesn't want me in his bed, in his kitchen tomorrow morning. And though it hurts, I understand.

When we arrive, I don't give him a tour and he doesn't ask for one. By the time the door closes, he already has my coat off and my shirt over my head. Yanking my bra upwards, he fills his hands with my breasts, relearning their curves, their weight.

"Ah, fuck me, you're still perfect," he mutters, and bends to cover one aching peak with his mouth. I grab his hair and arch my back with a cry, giving myself to the sensation. Giving myself to him.

We don't make it to the bedroom. I'd like to think it's out of desperate passion, but I know it's more than that. He doesn't want the intimacy of a bed. He wants me out of time and place, and that's okay with me. I want to give him what he needs.

His touch on my body is borderline savage, my own restraint just as absent. We aren't making love, too much heartbreak and betrayal between us. It's carnal war, selfish and needy.

I crawl naked onto my living room couch and grip the frame. James is a maelstrom of heat behind me, yanking me back from the cushions and crushing me to his chest.

"Tell me you want this," he growls.

"James—"

"Say it, Iris!"

"I want this. I want you. Please."

I don't stop begging until he tilts my hips and thrusts inside me in one smooth movement. Even primed by his mouth and fingers, I still shudder at the burning stretch that borders pain.

Some part of my James still lives, because he waits unmoving for me to adjust.

"Okay," I whisper.

With my consent given, he doesn't hold back. There's no finesse in his movements, no grace in my acceptance. Only the fierce sounds of flesh against flesh, of his grunts and my moans.

The fingers anchoring my hip spasm. "God help me," he gasps. "I can't... you feel—fuck!"

He empties inside me with hoarse cry, then immediately pulls out and stumbles back. The sudden withdrawal is shocking; I collapse against the couch, shaking and bereft. I don't need to see his expression to feel his regret.

His weight hits the coffee table with a thud. "We didn't use a condom," he says mutedly.

I lift my head just enough say, "I'll get the morning after pill."

"I'm, er, clean of disease, and I assume you—"

"Yes," I snap.

His sigh floats over my bare back. "Will you at look at me? We need to talk about this."

Grabbing a nearby blanket, I cover myself as best I can and turn around. What I see is both so right and *so wrong*. James, naked and flushed and beautiful, half-hard and glistening with sweat and me. But his face, his eyes—they aren't his.

I just had sex with a stranger.

"Just go," I say tightly. "You don't have to explain or placate me. I know what this was."

A brow quirks. "What's that?"

"Hate-sex."

Both eyebrows lift at that. "I don't hate you." He cocks his head thoughtfully. "Although the moniker is rather apt."

Pulling the blanket snug around me, I draw my knees to my chest and ignore the sensation of wetness leaking onto my couch cushions. I'll burn them tomorrow.

"What were you expecting, James? My tears? For me to beg you to stay?"

The sad fact is that I *would* beg if I thought it would do me any good. And I will cry—when he's gone.

He frowns. "No, I simply don't want you to misunderstand."

I laugh shortly. "Oh, I understand just fine."

His mask cracks for a moment. I see longing in his eyes, mixed with bright anger and old hurt.

"I loved you," he whispers. "Even if I never said it outright, you had to know."

Thinking it can't get any more painful than this, I throw caution to the wind and tell him the truth. "I did know, and I loved you, too. I still love you."

His eyes shutter, expression closing off. "Sorry pet,

the man you loved is dead, buried alongside the idealism of youth."

Oh, how wrong I was.

This is worse. Much worse.

A mirthless laugh scrapes from my throat. "Fucking poets. All of you are terminally narcissistic."

He stares at me in shock.

My own buried anger erupts. I point at him, uncaring that the blanket slips from my shoulders.

"Let's cut the flowery bullshit, Beckett. You lied to *me*. Methodically, flawlessly, over weeks and weeks. If anyone has a right to resentment, it's me. Face it—you're not angry with me, you're angry at yourself. You did this, not me. You didn't have the balls to see a disaster of your own making through to the end. *You* were the one who triggered my memory of the rape. You didn't fight for me, for us. You tucked tail and ran!"

"You told me you were seeing someone else!" he yells, jerking to his feet to pace across the living room. "You rejected me over and over. You were a fucking *ice queen*, Iris!"

My anger drains away, leaving me cold and hollow. I grab the loose blanket and cover myself as James yanks on his pants.

"Fuck, fuck, fuck," he chants. He grabs his shirt from the floor, then faces me with the fabric bunched in his hands. "We were loosely together, what, a grand total of three weeks? I can count on one hand the number of times we slept in the same bed. This is fucking ridiculous. A sick obsession I can't seem to rid myself of. You were right, what you told me back then. I loved a fantasy of you and for some reason, I can't let go of that woman. Even though she doesn't exist. Even when the truth invariably disappoints."

"Get the fuck out," I seethe.

"Gladly," he snaps, pulling on his shirt and stomping across the room for his shoes and coat.

A minute later, the front door slams. His car starts, tires squealing on the wet asphalt as he speeds away.

Quiet darkness retakes my world. I fold into myself, curling on my side with the blanket over my head.

***

When I don't answer Claire's repeated phone calls the following afternoon, she shows up and uses her house key to let herself in. She finds me still naked and nearly catatonic on the couch. At least I'm upright—the television is on and a half-eaten yogurt rests on the coffee table.

I blink lethargically. "How did you know I'd be here?"

She hands me a small brown pharmacy bag. "You don't remember texting me at six this morning?"

I peek inside the bag to see a little blue box. Memory—and sanity—returns in a rush. I tear open the package and pop the tablet from its sheath, gagging as I try to swallow it dry.

Claire shakes her head sadly, reaching into her purse for a water bottle. I chug until I can't taste the pill anymore, then hand the bottle back.

"It was Beckett, wasn't it?"

I nod.

"I take it things didn't end well?"

I snort. "You could say that."

"Do you want me to stay a while longer, Iris? I don't have to leave when Griff does, and I can just as easily job-hunt from here. I'll fly down for any interviews—"

"No, Claire. It's okay. I'll be okay."

Tears glisten in her eyes. "I'm worried. What are you going to do?"

My answering grin probably makes me look like a maniac, but I don't care. "Write the next Great American Novel, what else?"

28. mimesis

____

Three months later, on March 1st, my agent has a manuscript in her hands. It doesn't have a title yet and frankly, I'm not sure she'll even be able to pitch it. Dark and satirical, it's unlike anything I've written before.

On a whim, I email a copy to *j.s.beck*. I don't care if he reads it or not. I don't care if he loves it or hates it. And that's the point—I don't need him to build me up anymore, to bolster my writer's identity with praise or critique.

I don't need him.

A written purging of my demons, the finished novel is a reimagining of an obscure Scottish legend. Faintly dystopian and classically tragic, if it goes to print I'm guessing it will be thrown across rooms more than it's treasured.

It's not a happy tale.

"It's phenomenal!" yells the voice of my agent. "Depressing and heartbreaking and magnificent! I cried at least three times and you know how much I hate to ruin my mascara!"

My phone sits face-up on my kitchen table with the speaker on, bringing Rachel Tanaka's normally earsplitting tone to new heights. Allison grins at me from the chair opposite mine and mimics plugging her ears.

"Are you sure it's not too bleak?" I ask Rachel.

"No! Okay maybe, but I'm not sure I want you to change anything. I'll run it past the usual suspects, see what they think. I'll get back to you by the end of next week. Good?"

"Yes, thanks."

"Fabulous!"

The line goes dead.

Allison laughs. "She's one of those, huh? Who don't do goodbyes on the phone?"

I chuckle and nod. "She's a character."

Allison stands and stretches her arms over her head. "Are you sure you don't want to come tonight?"

"I'm sure. Thanks, though."

Every Friday, the café she manages, Tullamore, has an open mic night from seven until ten. I've gone a few times and enjoyed it, but watching a movie with my feet up and a glass of wine in my hand sounds infinitely better than sitting with strangers while Allison works. Even when some of those strangers are criminally sexy, flirtatious musicians.

Allison and I say goodbye at the front door. She runs down the short walk to her car, jacket over her head to keep the downpour off her curls.

A gust of wind sweeps rain under my porch roof and into my face. I jump back and close the door, wiping my eyes with the sleeve of my shirt. From the kitchen, I hear the muted buzz of my phone. Another buzz comes almost immediately, then a pause, and one more buzz.

Thinking it's Allison trying one more time to get me out tonight, I retrieve my phone and read the three short messages on the screen.

You wrote about selkies

FUCKING SELKIES!

I'm coming over

I drop the phone like it's bitten me. It bounces off the edge of the table and lands on the wood with a crack.

Three months and not a word. Three months to accept his absence in my life. Three months of letting go, of finding my own peace and happiness. Of feeling like a whole person, mature and confident.

I've even ventured into the dating world, the most recent contender a man I met at Bluebird Books. He's pursuing a PhD in Art History; funny, intelligent, and down-to-earth, he's taking me to dinner next weekend.

Three months...

...and I'll still beg for scraps from James Beckett's table.

I run into my bathroom and crank on the shower, scrambling out of my clothes and under the flow. The water's not even close to hot yet but I grit my teeth and wash myself head to toe. A razor in my shaking hand makes bloody work of my legs, though I manage to get my shit together for more delicate parts.

The water is just beginning to heat to bearable levels when I turn it off, jump out, and towel dry. I race across my bedroom and yank open my dresser, throwing leggings and a sweater on the bed.

"What's the hurry, pet?"

I scream and jump backward. My foot catches on an area rug and I'm falling, falling... until strong fingers clench on the knot of towel between my breasts and drag me upright. Viridescent eyes sparkle down at me in delight.

"Still a disaster," he murmurs.

Caught in the heart-shredding grip of adrenaline, I yell, "Jesus Christ! How did you get in!"

He grins. "You really shouldn't leave your front door unlocked." With a final tug on the knot, he releases me. "Put some clothes on, little muse. I'll brew us some tea."

I gape at him. He winks, then saunters from my bedroom, whistling a jaunty tune as he heads toward the kitchen.

"Are you kidding me right now?"

The universe doesn't answer.

Probably a good thing.

I tug on thick leggings, wincing at the sting from multiple small cuts on my legs. *Why did I bother?* Obviously we had completely different perspectives on what would happen if he came to my house. I'm an idiot. Since when has he ever done what I expect him to?

Over a bra and camisole, I pull on my rattiest, bulkiest sweater, then grab a hair clip from the top of my dresser. Not bothering with a mirror, I gather the damp strands onto the top of my head, wind them into a thick spiral, and clamp a portion with the clip's plastic teeth.

When I enter the living room, I find James looking

right at home on my couch, flipping through a book with his feet on the coffee table.

At my footfalls, he glances up. "You bought a new couch."

"Yes," I deadpan. "If you liked the old one, I believe it's still available for purchase from Goodwill. Fair warning—it's stained."

His eyes narrow, glinting with sharp humor. "Touché."

I cock an eyebrow. "If you wanted to give me feedback about the book, an email would have sufficed."

His lips twitch. "But then I would miss out on this enlightening banter."

"I wouldn't call it enlightening," I counter. "Tedious and oblique come to mind."

His grin is sudden and wicked, transforming his eyes, his face.

Transforming him into someone I know.

The man I loved.

James.

The kettle whistles softly, gaining in volume as we stare at each other. When it's loud enough to elicit winces from both of us, he finally stands.

Passing me on the way to the kitchen, he says, "Timing is everything, I suppose."

I agree.

I was fully prepared to meet him skin to skin, to lose myself in his arms. But if it's my heart he wants?

He's three months too late.

29. motif

"After all this time, you're still a mystery to me." I blow steam off the top of my tea. "Is that so?"

"Mmm." He takes a sip, then sets his mug down on the coffee table. "You're a study in contradictions. Despite my skill at chess, I still can't predict what you'll do."

That makes two of us.

I want to ask him what he wants, why he's here if not to appease our appetite for each other's bodies, but I don't. Perhaps I'm a bit of a masochist, myself. But at least part of the truth is simple—I enjoy his company. The wordplay, the verbal chess. Even with no sex involved, he's still the most brilliant, charming prick I know.

"I surprised you, the inimitable James S. Beckett. That's why you're here."

"Indeed. While I was reading your manuscript last night, it occurred to me that you didn't actually want or need me to read it." His eyes slant to mine. "True?"

Hiding my smile behind my mug, I nod.

"Then why did you send it?"

"Did you read the dedication?" I ask in return.

His eyes darken, lips tilting wryly. "Ah, I didn't want to assume that was for me." He chuckles softly. "Of course it is. *My little muse.* You certainly put me in my place, didn't you?"

I shrug, but my smile is pleased. "It was the least I could do. You gave me the idea, after all."

"I did, didn't I," he murmurs. "I suppose you know it's extremely morbid?"

"Selkie legends aren't known for happy endings," I say, not without irony.

He frowns, staring at his hands. "I guess I'm to blame for that as well."

I sigh, settling into the couch cushions with my tea cradled atop my stomach. "I don't think either of us is to blame. Things just... happen the way they're supposed to happen."

"Perhaps." He clears his throat. "I said things I didn't mean on New Year's Eve. I owe you an apology. Once again, you were right. I wasn't angry at you but at myself."

Mindful of our conversation veering in a dangerous direction, I keep my voice even and light. "Believe me, I get it. We were angry at ourselves, each other, whatever. That's why it's called hate-sex, James."

He laughs, sinking back with his arms crossed behind his head. I try to ignore the sliver of skin visible above his belt, but my eyes only move further south, snagging on the thick curve of him beneath soft denim.

Damnit.

I drag my eyes away and blink at the ceiling. "Can I ask a question without you getting weird?"

"That sounds interesting," he says brightly. "Fire away."

"That passage you read from *Indigo*, about the woman with the scar? Was it about me?"

"Of course. I wrote it after our first—and only— weekend together. You fell asleep on the rug before the fireplace after... anyway, I might have slipped the blanket off you to study you in the firelight."

I swallow hard, shifting subtly to alleviate the pulse of memory and desire between my legs.

"Sometimes I wish I was still her," I tell him. "That innocent girl."

"I never saw you as innocent." When he glances over

and sees my surprise, he smiles. "I know that's hard to imagine, but I've seen your childhood photos. At least the ones Richard kept. You were born with eyes that hold worlds. Lifetimes of love and loss and pain. I'm only sorry that I added to your pain. I truly never meant to hurt you."

"I know," I whisper.

He recites softly, "'*She lay still and hard and smooth before me, a chrysalises awaiting transformation. Soon, she would break free, and I would revel in witnessing her metamorphosis.*'" He smiles warmly. "Indeed, I've reveled in witnessing your metamorphosis."

Fighting a damnable stirring behind my eyes, I force a smile. "Am I a beautiful butterfly now?"

His smile softens. "You know you are."

There's a question in his eyes that I don't know how to answer, so I ask a different one.

"Is the novel too depressing?"

"Nah. Besides, depressing wins awards."

I laugh and kick his leg. "That's horrible advice."

He closes his eyes, lips curved in a smile. "In all honesty, I wouldn't change it past the usual edits. You misspelled dessert twice."

I jerk upright in horror. My empty mug rolls off my lap and thuds on the floor. "Shit, are you serious?"

He chuckles, nodding. "My favorite was, '*The desert

unfolded on her tongue.' A poetic take on dry-mouth, certainly."

Laughing, I cover my flaming cheeks.

James watches me with an impish grin. "Iris Eliot, you're blushing."

"Fuck off, Beckett."

"You didn't blush when I offered to bend you over, but you blush when I catch grammar errors? Good God, either you're a unicorn or I need lessons in seduction."

I swallow laughter, rolling my eyes. "You weren't even serious. Your *girlfriend* was waiting outside for you."

"Tsk tsk. No lying, pet. You and I both know why you looked at me like I was a cretin when I said it."

He can't possibly...

"Because I told you once that I'd only want you face to face."

Until this moment and those words, I didn't know it was possible for a heart to soar and sink at the same time.

"James..."

He waves off my cautionary tone. "Don't bother. Water under the bridge, eh?"

I repeat his own words back to him. "Is it, little muse?"

James laughs loudly and freely, the sound warming

me from the inside out. By the time he quiets, it's too late for me to hide the tears in my eyes.

Expression sobering fast, he sits up. "What's wrong, Iris?"

I shake my head and wipe at my traitorous eyes. "Nothing, really. I just realized how much I've missed you. Not the being with you part—that was a mess—just *you*."

"I'm a brilliant conversationalist, aren't I?"

I laugh, silently thanking him for lightening the mood. "And humble, too."

He nods. "Don't forget devastatingly handsome and impressively endowed. I don't suppose you'd fancy a shag?"

I groan. "Stop with the Austin Powers accent. You sound like a wanker."

He guffaws. "Did you just call me a *wanker?*"

"Yes. Yes, I did."

Eyes sparkling, he stands and collects our mugs. "You're right, of course. I'd better get going. I've got a serious wanking on the schedule tonight right after a wee wank or two."

I make a face. He laughs all the way to the kitchen, where he rinses the mugs and leaves them in the sink.

We meet at the front door. He pulls on his overcoat,

buttons it, and clears his throat. When he looks up, his eyes show me a rare glimpse of vulnerability.

"This is awkward," he mutters. "This is awkward, right?"

I laugh a little. "Yes. But I'm glad you broke into my house tonight."

He smiles. "Me, too. Lock the door behind me."

"Will do."

He nods, then surprises me by taking my face gently in his hands and kissing my forehead. Against my skin, he murmurs, "No matter what, you were my muse first."

Then he's out the door, jogging through the rain to his car. I wait until he starts the engine, then close the door and flip the deadbolt.

My forehead hits the wood, then my palms. Closing my eyes, I see again his final glance. The tenderness and warmth in his eyes. I think of how easy and right it felt sitting beside him, drinking tea and laughing.

And I wonder if timing really is everything.

30. objectivity

*S*pring makes a brief appearance the following week, and Friday night arrives cold but clear. At seven p.m., Peter the PhD candidate picks me up at Bluebird Books and takes me to sushi in Fremont. After sharing sashimi and rolls, we button our coats and walk the few blocks to Tullamore Café.

Over the course of our meal, I reconfirmed that Peter is considerate, smart, and charming. Moreover, conversation with him is easy, no intellectual pressure or emotional undertones to be found.

When he smiles at me and takes my hand, I smile back and let him. And for the rest of the walk to Tullamore, I privately bemoan the fact that his touch does absolutely nothing for me.

Strike one.

Inside the bright, warm café, we join the ordering line while a young woman strums a guitar on the nearby stage. The place is packed as usual, chairs and tables crammed together to accommodate the open mic night crowd.

As we near the front of the line, I spot Allison behind the espresso machines. She sees me at the same time and grins, eyebrows raised speculatively as she nods toward Peter. Pivoting away from my date, I give her a sad-face as a reply. With a half-amused, half-sympathetic smile, she returns to her task.

My attention now back with Peter, I realize he's ordered for me without bothering to ask what I want. Despite his thoughtful choice of a latte with whole milk —which I'd been drinking when we met—I'd wanted tea.

Strike two.

The third strike is so unexpected, so utterly mystifying, it almost feels orchestrated by powers beyond human comprehension. And whoever the powers that be are, they have a real fucked-up sense of humor.

It begins when I hear a laugh—*his* laugh—coming from somewhere behind me. At the same time, Peter takes his change and we move out of line. Then, as he's looking around for a place to sit, his eyes widen with awe.

And he says, "Oh my God, Iris, it's James Beckett.

Right there." His wide eyes meet mine. "Will you introduce us? I'm his biggest fan."

"Uhh—"

"Come on," he says, grabbing my hand and virtually dragging me toward the back of the line.

Strike three times a million.

"Well, well, well," drawls James, laughing eyes bouncing between my angry face and Peter's excited one. "If it isn't my former protégé. And who's this young man, Iris? Your newest acquisition? Tread carefully, boyo, *'though she be but little, she is fierce.'*"

I'm going to kill him.

Then I'll bring him back to life.

Then I'll kill him again.

Peter drops my hand like it's burning. "Mr. Beckett, it's such a pleasure to meet you. I'm a huge fan."

James' jaw clenches as he tries not to laugh. "I'm flattered," he says with strain.

Crossing my arms over my chest, I finally look at the woman standing flush to James' side. Jessica gives me a bland yet somehow venomous smile.

"Nice to see you again, Iris."

My only consolation is that she sounds like she's chewing glass. I'm so annoyed—by her, James, Peter, all of it—that a demon overtakes my vocal chords.

"You, too. Did you have a nice New Years? I know I did."

James stops talking mid-sentence. Peter keeps yammering like nothing's amiss, while Jessica stiffens in fury and spits daggers from her eyes.

I smile sweetly at her.

James clears his throat. Loudly.

"Iris, a word?"

Before I can say *Hell no*, he manhandles me out the front door with an arm locked around my shoulders. He marches us past the glowing windows and into a shadowed section of sidewalk.

"What the fuck was that?"

He doesn't sound angry. In fact, he sounds positively tickled. *Figures*.

I shrug, staring at the street. "I don't like her."

"Little muse, are you jealous?"

"No."

"Liar."

I ignore that. "Tell your biggest fan I was feeling sick and caught a cab home. Goodnight, James."

I start walking.

"Open relationship, remember?" he calls after me. "Say the word, pet, and I'll give you what you want!"

I turn, walking backward a few paces. "For such a brilliant man, you're pretty dense."

"What's that supposed to mean?"

"Ask Jessica!"

I spin and head for the nearest crosswalk.

He yells, "Shall I meet you at your house in, say, an hour?"

My middle finger lifts over my head. His merry laughter follows me across the street.

***

Sunday afternoon, I head to Bluebird Books with my laptop. Preliminary notes from my agency's top editor are in my email, but it's better I don't read them alone. With people around, I'll be less likely to throw temper tantrums.

My usual spot is taken, so I wander through the interconnected rooms for a bit of browsing and people watching. There are other open chairs and a few tables, but I'm a creature of habit. And I'm procrastinating.

On my third circuit around the store, the woman who occupied my chair is gone. Mildly disappointed, I slump into the armchair, pull out my laptop, and get to work.

An hour later, I slam the computer closed and rub my eyes.

"Are you stalking me, pet?"

"Jesus," I mutter, peering through my fingers. "Don't you live in Wallingford? There are bookstores closer to you."

James flops into the alcove's second chair. "Nope. Moved last year. A few minutes from here, actually."

My hands drop like rocks. "You're kidding."

He rolls his head toward me, sunlight making emeralds of his eyes. "You didn't wonder how I made it to your house so fast the other night?"

"No," I say, frowning. "Obviously I thought you were stalking me."

He grins. "Obviously. What are you doing?"

"Looking over an editor's notes on my draft."

"Oh good. I was hoping for some entertainment this afternoon. Last night was dreadfully dull."

I don't want to laugh. I really don't.

But I can't help it.

James watches my losing battle with a smile. "You know, life is so much easier when we obey instinct. It doesn't make you popular, of course, but it does make you free."

"The signature argument of a man who wants to fuck multiple women at the same time."

His brows skyrocket. "Don't hold back, love."

The word makes me flinch internally; I know it's a

colloquialism and doesn't mean what it implies. But damnit if it doesn't sting.

I give him a pointed look. "Just so we're clear, we're not going down that road again. But for the purpose of educating you, if we *were* going there, there's not a chance in hell I'd be okay with you having multiple partners."

He sucks his lower lip between his teeth, gaze darting between my eyes. Sunlight from the window behind us highlights the varying shades in his dark hair. A little grey is coming through at his temples, which naturally only adds to his appeal.

"Okay."

I frown. "Okay? Okay, what?"

"For the purpose of educating *you,* when we *do* go down that road again, there's not a chance in hell I'll want anyone but you."

My body goes taut and electric.

James smiles knowingly. "Guess I haven't lost my touch."

I glare, ignoring my warm face. "Don't say things like that just to prove a point. It's petty."

His smile vanishes and he nods. "You're right. I'm sorry."

"Who *are* you?" I blurt.

He winks and snatches the laptop off my lap. "Right

now, I'm your highly respected peer who's about to tell you whether or not your editor is full of shit."

Slipping a pair of reading glasses from his shirt-pocket onto his nose, he opens the computer. The email is already up and he wastes no time reading it.

Three hours later, we head to a café for dinner so we can continue our conversation. After, by some unspoken agreement we wind up in a nearby tearoom. We're the last customers, staying until we're booted out at eleven. Still talking, we take a long, meandering route to my house.

It's nearing midnight when he escorts me to my front porch and says goodnight. I wait for a kiss that doesn't come. He doesn't even hug me—hasn't touched me once in the last six-plus hours.

I know he feels it. The same chemistry we've always had. The excruciating sexual tension. The singular language our minds share.

I also know he's doing it on purpose. Toying with me, seeing how far he can push until I break.

He's playing me like chess.

I'm going to lose.

31. paradox

"I have something I need to confess to you."

I laugh at Claire's grave, worried tone. "Claire-bear, whatever it is, just tell me. Did you steal my favorite scarf when you left? I can't seem to find it—"

"I sent your letters to Beckett."

My hand abruptly stops chopping lettuce, and the knife releases from my nerveless fingers. It clanks onto the counter, spins toward the edge, teeters, then cartwheels toward my feet. Even facing potential amputation, I can't move—at this moment, if I lost a toe I doubt I'd even feel it.

Luckily, the knife embeds itself in the wood an inch from my ankle. I take a breath and release it slowly.

"I'm sorry, I just stepped into a parallel universe where my best friend told me she sent those letters."

"I'm so sorry," she whispers. "It was a mistake. A moment's insanity. I just started thinking about you and Beckett, and how you guys never really had a chance three years ago—"

"Holy hell, Claire McHenry!" I holler. "Are you insane? Do you have any idea what those letters *say?*"

"I read a few," she says meekly.

Feeling dizzy, I stumble to my kitchen table and sink into a chair. There isn't a word for what's going on inside me right now. It's a toxic combination of terror, shock, foreboding, humiliation, violation...

"I sent them four days ago to his office on campus," she says miserably. "Maybe you can intercept them?"

My mind races. "In a box?"

"Yes."

"Do you have a tracking number?"

"Um, I think so? Hold on, let me look."

I listen to her rummaging through papers, my anxiety spiking higher with every second. "I'm really mad at you, Claire. I don't—I can't even imagine what possessed you."

"I know," she moans. "If you never want to talk to me again, I'll understand. I'm so sorry!"

I sigh. "I know you are. Just find that fucking receipt."

"I got it! Yes!"

I grab a nearby pad of paper and pen. She recites the ridiculously long code, then I say it back to confirm.

"Iris, I—"

"I know you meant well," I interject, "but let me try to avert this disaster before we talk through it, okay?"

"Okay," she whispers.

I hang up. Every nerve in my body but one wants to throw the phone across the room, but my last nerve is the sane one. It reminds me that my laptop is in the bedroom, and I can use my phone to quickly look up the tracking info on the Box of Doom.

Fingers shaking, I manage to find the appropriate website and plug in the code. As the page loads, my feet pound a staccato rhythm on the floor.

Then I see them.

Two little words.

DELIVERED TODAY.

I'm halfway to my car before I realize I'm not wearing shoes. Hissing in frustration, I rush back inside and grab the closet pair that will do—my slippers—then I'm out the door again and jumping into my car.

I hit every red light between my house and the university, because apparently the powers that be still have it in for me. The sick bastards.

Once on campus, I swerve into the lot closest to the English Department. It's the middle of the afternoon and naturally there are no spots. So I do what any well-adjusted grown woman in this situation would do—park illegally in the slanted white lines at the end of a row. If campus security tows my car, Claire will be paying to get it out of impound.

My brother's oversized sweatshirt billows around me as I sprint toward the building. Panic supersedes any pain in my knee. I would run a fucking marathon right now if it meant I got those letters back before James opens them.

Bursting through the doors of the Department, I rush toward the back and into the corridor lined with faculty offices. For the first time today, luck is on my side —there's no one around to notice my frantic flight.

Skidding to a stop outside James' office, I yank open the top of his rectangular mail slot.

It's empty.

I wiggle the door's handle.

Locked.

My fist pounds the door before I slump against it and slide to the ground. Dropping my head to my knees, I gulp air in effort to calm my thundering heart.

Between breaths, I chant, "No, no, no."

A deadbolt clicks above me, the only warning

before the door swings inward. At the sudden loss of support, I roll backward and sprawl across the threshold.

An upside-down James grins at me.

"I was wondering when you'd show up."

For the past forty-five minutes, I've been sitting on the couch in James' office as he continues reading my letters. He's mostly silent, though every once in a while he'll snort or sigh.

I must be on an angelic hit-list.

When he's about halfway through the stack, he stops, folding the current letter carefully and placing it back in its envelope. His chair creaks as he leans back and crosses his arms over his chest.

The only scenario I can think of that might be as mortifying as this one is a high school nemesis reading your diary aloud to the entire class.

"Have you done any dancing since the accident?" he asks softly.

Nope, I decide. This is worse. Like having a thousand paper cuts in front of the one person in the world with salt and a vendetta.

"I really don't want to talk about it."

"You do know that most of what I've read, I already knew?"

"It's different," I grumble. "Totally different."

"What's so terrible about me reading them, Iris? Obviously you didn't write them yesterday." He pauses. "Has it occurred to you that this might be extremely meaningful for me? That reading how you felt about me then would provide some much-needed closure?"

I don't want closure, my heart whispers.

"No, I hadn't. But it still feels violating."

"Why? Because you think I'm going to use your private thoughts against you?"

I drag hands through my hair, knotting my fingers on top of my head. My gaze pings everywhere in the room but his face.

"No. Yes. Maybe. Not really."

He chuckles. "Rest easy, pet. I'll never use your love of 80s action flicks against you."

My lips twitch, my shoulders relaxing a fraction. He's right—much of what I wrote to him I later confessed in person. The other words, those about my feelings for him, are only scary because they're still true.

And I have no idea what to do about it.

James pushes back his chair and stands. "Come on, we're going on a field trip."

My eyes snap to his mischievous smile. "What? Where?"

He walks to the couch and extends his hand. "Up. I have a hankering for a chili-cheese dog with extra sauerkraut."

Laughter bubbles out of me. I take his hand and he draws me to my feet. "Derrick loved sauerkraut, not me. And I thought you said you wouldn't use any of this stuff against me."

"I'm not using it against you so much as I'm using it *for* me."

I frown. "What does that mean?"

He merely shakes his head, a private smile on his lips. Giving my fingers a final squeeze, he releases me and opens the office door.

"After you."

Frowning at the floor, I walk into the hall and wait as he locks up. When he gives the sleeve of my sweatshirt a playful tug, I look up into his clear eyes. What I see in them finally allows me to step outside my fear long enough to hope.

"James?" I whisper.

His gaze flickers to my mouth. "Not yet, little muse, but soon."

My heart thumps. Praying I'm not misunderstanding him, I echo, "Soon?"

His smile curls wickedly. "Very soon."

And just like that, the past and future collide. No explosions. No smoke or ash. No paper cuts or salt or pain at all.

We walk down the hall side by side, his stride slower to accommodate my shorter one. And although it maybe doesn't look perfect, to me it is.

"Iris Eliot, are you wearing *slippers?*"

32. parody

After our impromptu meal of chili-cheese hotdogs—which we discovered are surprisingly hard to find—I don't hear from James for two weeks. He'd told me he was going out of town, first to England to visit with his sister's family, then to New York to meet with his publisher.

I didn't really expect him to call every day or anything, but I'd hoped for *something*. An email, an occasional text... anything to keep at bay my rising uncertainty.

Some days, I want him so badly that I spend an embarrassing amount of time daydreaming about a life with him. Waking up every day to his face. Reading in a living room with Rufus on the couch between us.

Cooking and eating together. Brushing our teeth side by side.

Other days, dark questions cloud my mind. Why hasn't he called? Is he still seeing Jessica? Does he sleep with women besides her? Does he actually want a relationship, or is he stringing me along for the purpose of breaking my heart like I broke his?

For the most part I keep busy, filling my time with a second round of edits on my novel, taking a two-day trip to visit my mom, and seeing Allison a few times a week. Since Rose's marriage to Julian, the lead singer of Breaking Giants, and her subsequent pregnancy, we're kind of in the same boat of absentee best friends.

Not that either of us blame our friends or think they abandoned us. Quite the opposite, in fact. If it weren't for Rose and Claire making big changes in their lives, Allison and I probably wouldn't be developing such a deep, solid friendship.

On the Friday before James is due back in town, Allison sits on my couch flipping through television channels while I paint my toenails blue. We have a raucous evening planned—pizza delivery and a Nicolas Sparks movie marathon.

When Allison finally gives up on finding a channel with substance, she clicks over to the nightly news. I listen with half an ear to the depressing montage of tragedy and political commentary. Then I hear a name so unexpected that my fingers spasm and I paint a line of blue over the top of my foot.

"Turn that up," I tell Allison.

She does.

"Well-known New York defense attorney William Cabot has been the subject of a scathing, anonymous article in the New Yorker accusing him of raping sixteen-year-old Iris Eliot, daughter of poet Richard Eliot.

In her memoir, A POET'S DAUGHTER, Eliot details the assault, and though Cabot is never mentioned by name, our sources confirm that the two did date briefly just prior to the incident."

The other newscaster asks, *"If he did assault her, do we know why she never pressed charges, Monica?"*

"Our best guess, Paul, is that allegedly the only witness to the rape was Iris' older brother, Derrick Eliot, who died tragically that same night. The writer also mentions that due to drugging and trauma, she didn't have memories of the assault until more than a decade later."

Paul gives the camera a solemn look before turning back to Monica. *"What does this mean for William Cabot?"*

"Considered by his colleagues to be ruthless and driven, our sources tell us that Cabot was close to making partner at his firm. And while his firm refused to comment and Cabot himself isn't speaking with the media as yet, a PR nightmare like this one may certainly result in a parting of ways—

"Turn it off," I croak.

A second later, the screen goes black. Allison turns wide, anxious eyes to me. "It was him, wasn't it? William Cabot?"

I nod shortly.

"Who do you think wrote the article?" She pauses. "And do I need to kiss them or kill them?"

I ignore the question—the answer is too fucking painful—and lurch off the couch, racing to the kitchen for my phone. There are three missed calls: my mom, Claire, and Rachel Tanaka. I ignore two in favor of the person I was going to call anyway.

Rachel answers on the first ring. For once, her voice is close to a normal octave. "I've already talked to the publisher. A statement has been drafted denying your involvement in that fiasco of an article. It will roll on the morning news."

The words register, but I don't feel the relief I'd expected to. Instead, I feel a tornado of conviction take shape inside me. It spins upward, swallowing my feet, legs, torso, and finally my head.

Something inside me... shifts.

"No."

Rachel hesitates. "What? Did you just say no?"

"Yes, I said no. I don't want to deny anything. It was him, Rachel."

I hear her swiftly drawn breath. "Oh God, Iris. I'm so sorry. Fuck that piece of shit, then. Let me think about this." She mutters inaudibly for a few moments. "At worst, your publisher doesn't want to back you anymore. We should be prepared to fight a breach of contract lawsuit—bullshit about moral clauses and the like. I'll review it immediately. Are you thinking you want to make a statement in support of the article?"

"I don't know," I whisper.

"That's okay. We'll cross that bridge when we come to it. Right now, your silence is going to speak louder than words, anyway."

"I haven't, um—that is, did you happen to hear on the news, or know, whether Will has a family? Kids?"

"He's divorced. No kids."

Relief comes in a sweet wave. "Okay, thanks."

"Iris? Keep your chin up. And if you happen to know who wrote that article, don't tell me. But you should also give them a big kiss and a hug from me."

Chin up, buttercup.

I laugh weakly. "Thanks. Touch-base tomorrow?"

"You got it."

The line goes dead. I slump into a chair and stare listlessly at the dying herb garden on my kitchen windowsill. Allison's footsteps come up behind me.

"Why did I think I could grow herbs in winter?" I ask aimlessly.

She sits in the chair next to me. "I found the article online. Do you want to read it?"

I shake my head.

Two days later, I'm sitting in my mom's kitchen in Palo Alto. Her eyes are full of tears as she looks across the table at me.

"You *what?*"

"I asked him, baby. Two months ago, I found his card in a junk drawer from when he'd given it to me three years ago. I figured it was a sign that I needed to call and give him overdue thanks for the lovely book on your father. One thing led to another, and we started talking about you."

I pinch the bridge of my nose. "Tell me exactly what you said."

She drags in a heavy breath. "I told him that my one regret was that that despicable man would never be brought to justice through a trial."

"And what did he say?"

She gives me a watery smile. "He told me that words were weapons, too. So I said that if he ever came across a way to make such a weapon, I'd be grateful if he used it."

I close my eyes and sigh wearily, the insanity of the past two days finally catching up. I flew on a whim to California to escape, and inadvertently landed in another, no less mind-boggling cesspit of revelation.

I still haven't talked to James. I don't know if he's back in Seattle or still traveling. He hasn't called. I haven't, either.

"If you're going to be upset with anyone, it should be with me."

"I'm not upset," I tell her, opening my eyes. "I'm more confused than anything."

"Understandable, baby. I'm sorry you're going through this." She reaches out for my hand and I slip my fingers into hers. "Is there anything else you want to know?"

Did you have an affair?

I shake my head. "Nope."

*E*xactly one week after the article in the New Yorker, I get the news that my publisher isn't dropping me. For the millionth time, I say a prayer for gratitude that Rachel found me a liberal house to do business with. One who apparently has a firm, supportive stance on victim's rights. Furthermore, since I didn't write or endorse the article, in their eyes my professional reputation is unsullied.

Too bad not everyone agrees.

The P.O. Box listed for contact on my website is newly flooded with mail. Much of it is supportive and congratulatory, some of it hard-to-read commiseration from other victims of rape. But there's also a renewed influx of hate-mail.

After the third disgusting letter, I ask Kim to take

over my formerly enjoyable task of personally collecting and reading correspondence.

Just over three weeks have passed since I last saw or spoke to James. And finally, after a Sunday morning in which I do nothing but miss him, I grow a pair of Modern Woman Balls and use the phone.

"Hello, Iris."

My heart jumps to my throat, cutting off my ability to speak.

"By your silence, I assume you still want to throttle me."

I choke down racing pulse. "No."

"No?"

"I don't want to throttle you, at least not because of the article."

"Hmm. Did you read it?"

"Yes."

"And you don't hate me?"

"No."

"Then why do you want to throttle me, pet?" A smile comes through the words. "Dare I assume it's because I haven't called?"

"Why haven't you?" I blurt.

He pauses; when I hear a familiar creak, I realize he must be in his office on campus. "The truth? I was scared shitless you'd tell me off and never speak to me again."

I imagine his face frowning, his eyes soft with worry. I think of the countless times he's challenged me, enraged me, made me a better writer. A better woman.

"I've never taken you for a coward, James."

He sucks in a breath. "Iris?"

"Are you still seeing Jessica?"

He chuckles. "No. Not since the night of your jealous outburst."

I grin in spite of myself. "What are you doing tonight?"

"I'll pick you up at seven."

Checkmate.

---

*A*t quarter till seven, I step outside to wait for James. I've been showered, dressed, and ready for two hours, and I'm so nervous my armpits feel damp despite a fresh layer of antiperspirant.

Everything about this moment feels significant. Despite our past sexual history, we've never been on an actual date. Our initial attraction to each other always sat in conflict to his role as my professor. Already on volatile ground, our relationship had imploded at the first hint of conflict.

Granted, our conflicts had been of the extreme variety.

But he's not my professor anymore, and I'm not his slightly awed TA and student. He's my professional peer. And more importantly, I no longer feel less talented, less mature, less capable than him. I know full well that he never made me feel that way—if anything, he insisted the opposite was true. I also know that my fears played a large role in our demise.

"Butterfly, butterfly," I chant under my breath. "You're a beautiful-effing-butterfly."

The affirmation alleviates some of my emotional jitters, softening jagged edges with humor. When I see his car turning the corner nearest my house, though, I almost throw up.

He pulls up to the curb outside my house and rolls down the passenger window. "Don't even think about running inside right now. I'll break down that door and throw you in the trunk if necessary."

Shocked laughter bursts out of me. This man is seriously too smart for his own good.

His teasing smile pulls me toward him as surely as a rope. Within a minute, I'm inside the car and buckling my seatbelt. I'm grateful to see that he's wearing jeans, and even more grateful I'd followed instinct and not worn a dress.

"Nervous, eh, pet?"

I roll my eyes. "Don't rub it in."

He chuckles and puts the car in drive, then pulls away from the curb. "If it helps at all, I'm nervous, too. But more in a what-are-the-chances-I'm-getting-laid-tonight sort of way."

I groan-laugh. "Still such a prick."

"Undoubtedly," he agrees, "but you don't look green anymore. I suppose that makes me a brilliant prick."

I smile, turning my head to see where we're going. He's not driving toward the bustling streets of Capitol Hill or in the direction of downtown, but east into an older, more affluent neighborhood.

Excitement brings me upright. "Are you taking me where I think you are?"

He glances at me with a soft smile. "I thought there might be someone you'd like to see." When I nod happily, he laughs. "He'll be very glad to see you, too."

Before long, he pulls the car into a short driveway before a modest gate. Rolling down his window, he punches a series of numbers on a keypad.

I gape at what lies beyond the gate. Huge trees create a picturesque frame for the stately home, grey with white trim and navy front door. Unlike the newer construction of his prior home, this one looks like it's seen a century or so, and aged more gracefully than any of us can hope for ourselves.

"Are you shitting me right now?"

He drives through the gate and into a carport nestled against the side of the house. "Unlike other things, it's smaller than it looks."

I slap his shoulder for the bad joke, then hasten out of the car, beating him to the side door in my anticipation.

He laughs. "It's just a house."

"Whatever. I have a thing for old houses. Just let me geek out, okay?" Something heavy thumps against the other side of the door. "Rufus!"

He barks, then whines.

Without further ado, James unlocks the door. Although I take a step forward, I don't actually make it into the house. Rufus jumps faster than James can grab for him. Eighty pounds of muscle and fur slam into me at the same time a slobbery tongue finds my neck.

After stumbling back a few steps, I regain my footing. Rufus continues licking my neck and face as I rub my hands vigorously over his sides.

"Oh, that's a good boy. Yes, you are. The best boy. I knew you loved me more than your daddy. I missed you too, buddy."

Standing with one hand braced on the doorframe, James laughs until tears leak from his eyes.

34. subtext

Rufus won't leave my side as James gives me a tour of the three-bedroom home. The interior has been beautifully renovated into a modern writer's retreat. Serene and inviting, the space reeks of James' singular presence.

It's no effort to imagine him inspired here; nor is it hard to see his inspiration manifested. The restored wood floors, elegant grey walls, and crisp white molding provide a stunning backdrop for bold paintings and eclectic flotsam he's collected over the years.

I hadn't realized how barren his Wallingford home had been, thinking he preferred an uber-minimalist approach. When I mention the thought aloud, he chuckles knowingly.

"I'm actually a bit of a packrat. The majority of my things were in storage for my first year here."

I arch a brow. "Weren't sure U-Dub would stick?"

He shrugs, turning to open a door at the end of a hallway. "I wasn't sure about a lot of things back then. I thought you might like to see this room in particular."

As I walk into the shadowed interior, he flips a wall switch.

"I'm dead and this is heaven," I breathe.

A library.

The walls to either side of me are covered in floor-to-ceiling bookshelves, nearly every shelf full. Directly ahead of me is his desk, set inside a spacious alcove and facing a large bay window. No curtains mar the view outside; though I can't see much, I have the impression of lush greenery.

"This is what sold it for me."

"Damn right it did."

James smiles and watches me browse the nearest shelves.

"Are you hungry, pet?"

"A little, yeah." Rufus' tail starts thumping. I stroke his head, laughing as I look up at James. "Honestly, I can't believe he remembered me."

James tugs a hand through his hair, expression

sheepish. "I might of, uh, found a t-shirt you left at my old place. It's since become Rufus' favorite blankie."

My eyes widen. "Rufus sleeps with one of my t-shirts?" His lips twitch as he nods. "But it's been three years! You had to have washed it since then, right?"

I'm rewarded by a faint flush on his cheekbones. "You're not going to let me out of this one, are you?" he murmurs.

"Nope. Not even a little bit. Spill."

He looks at the ceiling and mumbles, "I might have purchased a bottle of your perfume."

A warm, weightless feeling expands inside my heart. "James Beckett, you bought my perfume to spray on Rufus' t-shirt blankie so he wouldn't forget me?"

He winces. "When you say it like that, it sounds rather pervy, doesn't it?"

"No," I say softly. "It sounds hopelessly romantic."

His gaze lowers to my face. "What can I say, I'm a poet." And though the words are flippant, the look in his eyes is anything but.

Heat dances in my chest and belly, sinking lower and intensifying. My expression causes him to close the distance between us in two long strides.

"I'm going to kiss you now, Iris."

He doesn't wait for a reply—not that one is required.

There's nothing in the world I want more in this instant than his mouth on mine.

The touch of his fingers on my face is featherlight, trailing across my jaw and up cheeks, and finally sinking into my hair. With a gentle tug, he draws me forward until my aching breasts meet his chest.

His eyes, dark with desire, meet mine. "I've waited lifetimes for this."

"Me, too," I whisper.

He kisses me then, softly and sweetly. A delicate mingling of our breaths. We savor. We tease. His tongue flicks against my lip and I shiver, a moan fluttering in my throat.

More. More. More.

A shove from behind rocks me forward, smashing my lip against James' teeth. Sharp pain shatters my pleasure.

"Ow, fuck." Stumbling back, I prod at my throbbing upper lip.

"Rufus, heel!" admonishes James. His concerned gaze swings to me. "Are you all right? Do you need ice? Are you bleeding?"

I shake my head, fighting a smile. "I'm okay."

Rufus whines in uncertainty, his tail thumping and dark eyes inquisitive on my face. My pain forgotten, I drop to my knees and open my arms to accept a joyful, slobbery doggie hug.

Visible over Rufus' shoulder, James smiles and shakes his head. "I've created a monster, haven't I?"

I give Rufus a final squeeze before releasing him. "I like my monster, thank you very much."

Chuckling, James reaches for my hand. "Come on, let's get some food."

We walk to the kitchen, its counters bare and glistening. "You need to learn how to cook, Beckett."

"Why bother? I'll just buy you some lessons."

Leaving my side, he rummages in a drawer and pulls out several restaurant menus. He eventually notices my silence and glances over his shoulder with a grin.

"Don't tell me you've forgotten your line?"

I'm blank for a moment, then recall comes in a flash. "Sod off, you misogynistic prick!"

He nods approvingly. "Thai or Pizza?"

Two hours later, I sink onto the living room couch with my arms cradled protectively over my stomach.

Lips pinched to contain laughter, James settles beside me. "Are you all right?"

I groan for the third time.

His smile fades as he studies my face. "You don't look well, pet."

"I think I'm dying," I moan. "Death by pizza."

His lips twitch, but the concern doesn't leave his eyes. Gently, he places the back of his hand on my forehead. I watch his expression veer from worry to alarm.

"Be right back."

My eyes fall closed as his weight lifts from the couch. Minutes or hours later, he tugs open my mouth and tucks a thermometer under my tongue.

"Ughh," I whine.

After a little beep, the thermometer retracts. "Uh oh, you've a nice little temp."

"What is it?"

"101."

"Shit." I struggle to sit up but the room spins wildly. "I think I'm going to—"

That's all I get out. Besides pizza.

Lots and lots of pizza.

When the contents of my stomach lining join the horror-show already on the coffee table, James picks me up and carries me upstairs.

"Puked on you," I mumble, too numb to feel much besides mild annoyance.

His chest vibrates as he chuckles. "I thought I was in a remake of the *The Exorcist* for a minute there."

Humiliation spikes through my mental fog. "Oh God. Kill me now."

He carries me across a shadowed room into a bathroom. "Not a chance. But you do need a bath, and cool water will help your fever."

My head falls listlessly to his chest. "So sorry."

"None of that now," he says softly.

He sets me down on the lip of a massive tub and crouches before me, putting his hands right on my puke-spattered knees.

"Look at me, love."

Still in control of my eyeballs, at least, I look up at him miserably.

"There's no one on earth I'd rather be puked on than you."

Despite my pervasive ickiness, I manage a snort. "You can take me home. Don't want to get you sick."

James gives me a look of astonishment. "Are you nuts? Pass up the opportunity to have you at my mercy? Not a chance."

He gives me a kiss on the forehead and moves to turn on the faucets in the tub. Leaning against the tiled wall beside me, I decide that if this is being at James Beckett's mercy, I'm 100% on board.

35. surrealism

"**L**et me get this straight. You puked on him, then he bathed you, clothed you, and babied you for a day and a half, even calling in sick to work so he could hand-feed you soup and take your temperature every hour?"

"Um, yes."

Claire screeches into the phone, "Why are you ignoring his calls, you dummy?"

"Because!" With a grunt of aggravation, I flop onto my couch. "Claire, I don't know how to do this."

Something in my voice softens her outrage. "Honey, I know it's scary. You've never tackled a relationship-ready man before. But you're also the bravest woman I know. It's obvious Beckett is nuts about you. He sprayed his dog's toy with your perfume, for fuck's sake!"

Back to outrage.

"It was my t-shirt," I mumble.

"Exactly!"

"But I puked on him! Bits of cheese and pepperoni all over his lap! His coffee table! His rug! Bathroom! Sheets!"

"And he loved it!" she hollers back. "Iris, seriously, don't make me get on a plane. I will haul you to his house and throw you naked into his front yard."

I frown. "Geez, Claire. That's a little extreme."

"Yeah," she agrees in a normal tone. "What can I say, I felt inspired. Besides, I don't have any more letters to send him."

"Bitch," I say tiredly.

"Whatever, you forgave me because it was awesome." She pauses. "What are you really afraid of? He knows almost as much about you as I do and he's not running."

I stare out my living room window at the steady rain. "I don't really know," I murmur. "It's kind of this amorphous feeling of dread, like any second the other shoe is going to drop. I'm scared."

"Can I give you my professional two-cents?" she asks hesitantly.

"Yeah."

"Beckett's a poet and a writer. He calls you his muse. Does that remind you of anyone?"

I close my eyes. "My parents."

She hums in agreement. "I think you need to find out the truth about what happened between them. You need to talk to your mom."

The feeling of dread inside me grows, triggering goosebumps along my arms. "I don't want to," I whisper.

She sighs. "I know, honey, but you have to, or you're never going to be able to go all-in with Beckett. Or anyone else, for that matter. Regardless of what your mom says, you'll have to make a decision. But at least you'll be making one with all the facts."

"You're right." I sigh. "I think some part of me has always known that was the issue. I'll go see my mom next weekend."

"What about Beckett? And don't say you can't face him because of puke. Griffen took a shit with the bathroom door open the other day. This isn't the minor leagues of relationships anymore, when we pretended people didn't fart. We're in the majors now."

I laugh in spite of myself. "Ignoring that gross fact, did you really just use a baseball analogy?"

"Ugh, I know. You wouldn't believe how crazy Texans are about sports. It's rubbing off on me." A door opens and closes. "Gotta go, my client's here. Love you, Iris."

"Love you, too."

I lower my phone to my lap. Seconds later it buzzes with a new text message. From James.

Open your goddamn door

"Iris!" shouts James from the other side of the wood. "I know you're in there. I swear on the Queen of England I'll break this door down if you don't open it!"

I don't give myself time to think—I follow the soaring of my heart and run to the door. When I swing it open, James' fist halts mid-flight.

I clear my throat. "Hi."

He sighs heavily, lowering his arm. "Christ, woman. You're going to put me in an early grave. Why haven't you answered your phone?"

I open my mouth but nothing comes out. Standing before me windblown and worried, he's so beautiful that my breath is taken away. His hair is damp from the rain, plastered against his temples. Beneath furrowed brows, his eyes are dark, forest green.

I find my voice. "Would you accept it if I say I can't talk about it right now, but I'll tell you soon?"

His brow clears even as his eyes narrow. "On one condition. You invite me inside and feed me dinner and let me hold your hand while we watch whatever ridiculous action movie you want."

Warmth surges through me, bright and encompassing.

"Okay, but I have one more condition."

"Yes?"

"Before dinner and a movie, you take off my clothes."

The last of his worry dissolves as his eyes brighten. "Sex before a date? You modern woman, you."

Laughing, I grab the lapel of his coat. "Get in the house."

We don't watch a movie. We barely eat dinner, too hungry for each other to notice. We christen my new couch, the kitchen table, and end up listless and replete on the soft rug in front of the fireplace.

"Someday we'll make it to a bed, right?" I ask sleepily.

He kisses my shoulder. "Beds are for ordinary lovers. And we're anything but ordinary."

Rolling onto my back, I look up at him. "Inflated ego, much?"

A soft smile curls his lips. "Whenever will you learn, little muse? In every way, you're extraordinary."

His eyes and fingertips trail lightly between my breasts and down my stomach. I'm too blissed-out to mind when he begins tracing the various scars on my torso. Some are smooth and thin, some thicker and slightly raised, having been deep enough to need stitches. When his attention shifts to my right side, where the skin is thicker and whorled from burns, his eyes come back to mine.

The intimacy of being emotionally and physically bare hits me hard. And while I know I'm safe with him—the desire in his eyes tells me as much—it's still a battle not to reach for the nearby blanket and cover myself.

"Iris," he whispers. "So aptly named. Complex and radiant, deceptively delicate. Did you know why your parents named you that?"

I nod. "Not the flower, the Greek goddess."

He smiles as his hand travels south, flirting over my belly button and teasing the apex of my thighs. "And did you know the goddess was considered a link between heaven and earth, that she guided souls to paradise?"

I roll my eyes. "Please tell me you're not going to say my vagina is a link to heaven."

He chuckles, because that's exactly what he was

going to do. Lowering his head, he places a soft kiss on my breast as his fingers sink between my legs.

Arousal trips through my system, bringing my back off the floor in a languid stretch of desire.

"Heaven," he whispers as he shifts above me.

As he settles between my legs, I lock my ankles around his waist. I don't have to tell him how sore I am; he knows, entering me one slow inch at a time. As the delicious feeling of fullness intensifies, for the third time tonight I thank God for IUDs. Nothing in my life has prepared me for the soul-wrenching sensation of nothing between us.

James drops his forehead to mine. "Give me words, little muse. I need them. I need to know you feel what I feel."

I arch beneath him, striving to pull him deeper. "I'm yours, James," I whisper against his lips. "For better or worse, I've always been yours."

His mouth veers to my neck as he draws back, then sinks inside me again. "God, I hope you mean that. I'm not letting you go again. You're mine."

For how long?

I ignore the fearful whisper in the back of my mind, locking it beneath the here and now—the steady, swirling thrusts of his hips, the sweet, stretching burn, the way our bodies move together so effortlessly.

It's poetry. Pure and perfect.

I cling to it, memorizing each small sensation. The whisper of his stomach against mine. His scent, surrounding me. Our sweat, mingling. Our tasting tongues and sighs. The skillful press of his thumb on my clitoris as he drives me to yet another shattering peak.

All the wordless languages of our love.

And I pray they will be enough.

On Wednesday, I call my mom to plan a visit. She excitedly informs me that Phillip and Victoria are going on a father-daughter trip the coming weekend. Despite the synchronicity, this time I have no sense of higher powers colluding, either for me or against me. I respond to the news with equal eagerness; as Claire said, it's time to find out the truth.

Armed with memories of the last two nights with James, as I board the plane I'm not anxious but coolly determined. I spend the brief flight writing him a letter, in it promising that nothing my mom says will change my heart.

Palo Alto is unsurprisingly warm and sunny. My mom and I spend Saturday doing things we rarely did when I was young—getting massages, manicures, and facials. Our conversations are light, revolving around mundane things like recent movies and books, and what we want for dinner.

At my request, she cooks my favorite homemade lasagna, and we eat on the back deck while the sun is setting. The bottle of wine on the table is mostly gone, and I can see by the softness in her eyes that now's the time.

It's time.

"Mom, I need to ask you something about dad."

My soft words hover in the space between us. I see the moment they sink in—her shoulders stiffen minutely. For the first time, it occurs to me that she knew this day would come.

"Of course, baby. Anything."

Now that the moment's upon me, words clog my throat and tangle on the way out. "The locked box in your nightstand, the letters that dad found—was that... did it—"

"Are you asking if I had an affair like Richard thought?"

She doesn't sound insulted, but tired beyond her years. I nod. "Yes, I am."

She takes a sip of her wine, then sets the glass down. I watch her fingers twitch and curl around the stem. "You're back with James Beckett, aren't you?"

Foreboding shivers down my spine. "Yes. Why does that matter?"

Meeting my eyes, she smiles slightly. "You were my cautious child. My thoughtful, introspective Iris. So perceptive, so sensitive." Her gaze goes unfocused. "Derrick was the wild one. My risk-taker. My freedom-seeker."

"Mom?" I ask softly.

She shakes her head a little, eyes refocusing on my face. "When your father and I met, I was in love with someone else. But love's a funny thing—I fell in love with Richard, too. Can one love eclipse another? It certainly felt that way. When I was with Richard, the world was brighter. Everything was clearer, more vibrant. Poetic. I loved him because I didn't have a choice. Do you understand?"

"Yes," I whisper.

She nods. "Having met James, I think you truly do. They are very similar, you know. Minds like razors, smooth as silk and at the same time so sharp that when you're cut, you don't feel pain at first. Richard, as you know, was mercurial to a fault. A hopeless romantic who wanted a family more than anything. But he was also a narcissist and struggled with feeling like he couldn't love both his family and poetry. He felt that whichever passion he chose at any given time, an equally vital piece of his life was being smothered."

I have no idea where she's going, but from her wistful tone it's nowhere I've considered. The thought doesn't comfort—it scratches at the surface of my buried fears, bringing them alive.

She finishes her wine in two long swallows. The glass hits the table with a dissonant clank.

"Something not many people know about your father was that he believed strongly—profoundly—in the sanctity of life. He also wanted a large family. At least five kids, as he often told me. But there was a disparity, obviously, between his fantasy and reality. I was raising you and Derrick virtually alone. When Richard chose us, was emotionally present for us, he was magnificent. A perfect partner and father. When he chose poetry..." She shrugs.

"I remember," I say mutedly.

And I do, primarily the inconsistency. The not knowing if the man walking in the door at night would be my dad or a stranger with his face. One who didn't want hugs and kisses and bedtime stories, but who disappeared into his study for hours at a time.

With a sigh, she tells me the rest.

"That weekend I disappeared, I went to Los Angeles

to visit a female friend from college. She went with me to a clinic so I could get an abortion."

My breath stalls. For a few moments, my mind is blank with shock. *Definitely* not an avenue I'd considered.

At length, I ask, "Will you tell me why?"

"I was in a dark place, barely able to care for myself while trying not to fuck up you and Derrick."

"You were—are—a great mom," I say firmly.

She smiles sadly. "I tried. But when I found out I was pregnant, that my birth control had failed, I couldn't fathom another child. Not with our marriage beginning to fall apart, with his absences on tours and speaking engagements growing more frequent and longer. So many times, Richard promised to be more present, to stay invested, but he couldn't." She shrugs a shoulder. "He tried. He really did. But he just couldn't do it."

Tears fill my eyes and I reach for her hand, squeezing it tightly. "Oh, mom. I'm so sorry. That must have been so lonely for you."

"Yes, it was. And believe me, Iris, I didn't want to deprive you or Derrick of a sibling. I honestly didn't feel like I had a choice."

"Why didn't you tell him?" I ask at length.

She sniffles, releasing my hand to wipe at her eyes. "I was young and afraid. As progressive as he was on some counts, Richard didn't believe in abortion. In my darkness and confusion, I thought he'd feel my decision was more of a betrayal than infidelity." She sobs quietly, stifling it with her arm. "There isn't a day that goes by that I don't wonder if things would have turned out differently had I just told him. For all of us."

I know she means Derrick, and to lesser extent me. What if a third child had changed my father? What if he'd become the positive, loving presence we'd once known? Would that night have happened? Would I have sought love from someone who ultimately took advantage of me? Would I have been raped, and would Derrick have died?

What if, what if?

"I'm sorry, Iris," whispers my mother.

As I look at her, I feel no resentment. Only sympathy for her pain. "You don't have anything to apologize for, mom. But can I ask another question?"

"Of course."

"Why did you keep the letters from your high-school sweetheart?"

"If my love for your father was a summer thunderstorm, my love for Phillip was a steady spring rain. It was often overshadowed by the beauty of lightning, but in the end it lasted longer."

"Phillip?" I echo in shock. "*The* Phillip? My stepfather?"

She nods. "I never wrote him back while I was married to your father. It's important to me that you know that." She waits for my nod before continuing. "By the time Richard and I divorced, Phillip had married and moved away. But nine years ago, we ran into each other at the grocery store of all places. And I found out his wife had passed away from cancer five years before, and he'd moved the girls back here."

"The timing was finally right."

She smiles softly. "You could say that, yes."

Sitting back in my chair, I close my eyes and try to absorb everything I've just learned. The unmet potential of a sibling. My mother's fear and difficult choice. The conflict of two loves. For her it was two men. For my father, love and art. What all of this means for myself, my heart, and my love for James.

Is he like my father? Can he give himself equally to a partner and to his passion? But the more important question is, *Can I let go of the past in order to embrace the future?*

There's only one way to find out.

37. transition

My mom and I enjoy a low-key Sunday. We relax, watch movies, and laugh a lot. With yesterday's confession behind us, she seems lighter, unencumbered by at least one of the regrets she's carried for so long. She's still a woman of many layers, but not so mysterious anymore. And infinitely more beautiful because of it.

On the flight home, I put the truth in black and white as I finish my letter to James. Giving both myself and him the resolution we sought three-and-a-half years ago. The truth about the weekend my mother disappeared, which changed the course of my father's life and all of ours. A truth both less sensational and more momentous than expected.

After we land and I collect my car from longterm

parking, I drive straight to the place my heart sings for. To him.

When I'm getting off the freeway, I call to make sure he's home. And when he doesn't answer, I figure he's writing and I have the unique opportunity to surprise him. I stop at my favorite Thai place and grab takeout, then drive to his house.

As I pull up, I'm surprised to see the driveway blocked by an idling cab. The gate stands open, James' car in the port. The first tendrils of fear rise but I shove them down, unwilling to be controlled by doubts. There are hundreds of logical explanations for a cab being parked outside his house.

Right? Right.

Parking against the adjacent curb, I grab the food and lock up my car, then head toward the driveway. The cab's window is down, so I wave hello.

The cabbie tips his head. "'Evening."

I glance at the house, at James' BMW in the carport. "Are you picking someone up?" I ask, because it'd be rude to ask if he has the right address.

"Yep. Lady called a half-hour ago. I'm a few minutes early."

My fingers and toes go cold and numb. The tendrils of fear become thick, suffocating vines. "A lady?" I repeat weakly. "Did you catch her name?"

The cabbie's eyes narrow. "Nuh uh, not going there." He points at the house. "If your man is in there with another chick, I want no part of it."

I force a smile. "Understood. Have a good night."

One difficult step at a time, I walk up the driveway to the side door. *Please, please, please.* I don't know what I'm asking for. Mercy, maybe. A swift end to my misery.

The hum of anxious blood in my ears, I press the little silver doorbell.

And wait... and wait.

A little voice whispers, *Just leave. Walk away.* I tell it to shut up and press the doorbell again.

Rufus barks somewhere in the house.

Finally, I hear a voice. A female voice. "Coming!" she calls, then says more softly, "Cab's here, James. Call me tomorrow?"

I hear his voice but can't make out the words.

Frozen, I watch the door open. Stare at the woman who stops abruptly. Her eyes widen as she recognizes me, then a slow smile spreads across her face.

"Well, well," Jessica purrs. "If it isn't the prodigal student. Still stalking your professor, *pet?*"

In lieu of throwing a bag of food in her face—or better yet, a can of gasoline and a lit match—I turn around.

Walk down the driveway.

Get in my car.

Start the engine.

Pull away from the curb.

Drive past the cab.

Drive.

Drive.

Drive.

U-turn.

Accelerate back the way I came.

I'm done running.

———

I hold down the doorbell until I hear Rufus going berserk, loud footsteps running, and James' angry voice muttering about skinning someone alive.

The door swings open. "What the fuc—" Shirtless and dripping from an interrupted shower, James blinks at me in stupefaction. "Iris? What's the matter?"

"Hi, James. You said you weren't seeing Jessica anymore."

He frowns. "I'm not."

I guess I'm angrier than I feel, because I have to clench my hands to keep from slapping him. Or strangling him. Or trying to take a bite out of his neck.

"I want the truth," I grind out between my teeth. "Was all of this just to get back at me for three years ago? Make me fall in love with you again so you could rip it all away?"

He crosses his arms as a breeze picks up. Goosebumps lift across his chest. "What the hell are you talking about? Jesus, it's cold. Will you come inside?"

"Nope. Tell me the truth. Did you fuck her today, when she was at your house?"

Confusion.

Dismay.

Comprehension.

Anger.

"Are you kidding me? For fuck's sake, is it always going to be like this?" He pauses, eyes smoldering. "Will you ever trust me?"

Doubt stirs through my rage like heavy ink, cooling and dampening. I recall Jessica's smart business attire, her perfectly coiffed hair, and the crisp lines of her lipstick. Had she looked like a woman just fucked? No, she hadn't.

"I want to trust you," I say in a more reasonable tone. "But you told me you weren't seeing her, and I brought you dinner, and she answered the door, and... and... she's such a bitch!"

He bites his lips but can't disguise the laughter brimming in his eyes. "Unfortunately, Jessica was the architect I hired to help with renovations when I bought the house. She was here yesterday to finalize the transfer of the remaining work to one of her associates. You must have just missed him. His name is Gerald. Trim fellow, very tall. Has a mustache like a circus ringleader."

I manage, "Oh."

"You brought me dinner?"

"It's probably cold now."

He grins. "I have a microwave."

I wince as I meet his eyes. "You don't hate me?"

"Not even remotely."

"Okay. I'm sorry. I'll, uh, go get the food." I turn away, but his voice stops me.

"Iris? You realize I heard you, right? The bit where you said you're in love with me again?"

Heart hammering, I face him. *No more running*. I meet his gaze, sober and soft now.

"Of course I love you, Beckett. I've always been in love with you, and I probably always will be."

His smile blooms like a sunrise, slow and dazzling. He nods toward my car. "Go on, then, before I catch pneumonia."

My brows skyrocket. "You're not going to say it back?"

James chuckles, infinitely pleased with himself. "I

will, just not right this second." He glances at an imaginary watch on his wrist. "You have to wait, oh, give or take forty-five minutes. Long enough for my balls to thaw."

"Wow," I deadpan.

He winks.

Forty-five minutes later, we've eaten and opened a bottle of wine, and he still hasn't told me he loves me. Of course, James is visibly tickled by my growing disgruntlement and makes me sweat it out for another fifteen minutes.

Then he says, "I want to show you something." Rufus and I follow him to the study, where he points to a large cardboard box sitting on the floor next to his desk. "Take a look inside."

Curious and not a little confused, I lower to my knees and open the top flaps. At first, I don't know what I'm looking at. All I see is my name in sloping white text emblazoned on satiny black.

Six of my names.

On six identical covers of identical books.

His name, in a more subdued font, is beneath the title.

The *title*.

"You wrote a book of poetry about me," I whisper. "This is the book you were talking about at the signing."

"Ask me when I wrote the first poem."

Blinking tears from my eyes, I turn. "When?"

"Six years ago, when Richard first told me about his daughter."

I stand up. "And the last?"

"There will never be a last, little muse. You have my heart, my soul, and whatever afterlife waits for me. You are the first and the last. I need you, and I will never choose poetry over you. You *are* my poetry. I love—"

I swallow the rest of his words with a kiss.

Epilogue

JAMES

Scotland is bloody cold. Yes, I realize how ridiculous that sounds coming from a native Brit, but holy hell, the first Pict who set down his spear in this Godforsaken land and called it home must have had the worst sense of direction born to man. Either that, or he was a dolt.

And clearly so am I for subjecting myself to my third—and final, damnit!—winter in Edinburgh. Thankfully, there's a light at the end of the tunnel, and the name of that light is tenure at Stanford University in California. You know, where the sun shines and my balls don't crawl up to my throat every time I step outside?

I can't fucking wait.

"Such a baby," coos the object of my endless obsession and the reason I'm here to begin with.

A long strand of pale hair falls over my shoulder. I give it a little tug until she presents her cheek for me to kiss.

"I told you that you're not allowed to read my journals until they're at least a year old."

"Because you think that given enough time, I won't be offended by the shit you write. And I've reminded you on several occasions that your reasoning is bullshit. I'm *still* pissed about the Maldives incident."

I rock back in my desk chair, tilting my head to see her face. She's got the stern expression down pat, but I've always been able to see right through her. There's amusement in her selkie-dark eyes.

Playing along, I offer my most innocent mien for her viewing pleasure. "For the thousandth time, pet, when you asked me to pack your *mac*, I thought you meant a raincoat. Despite what I said in my journal, I assure you it was only after the fact that I realized you meant your computer. Where I'm from, macs are waterproof jackets."

Iris knows I'm lying, of course, and her lips do a precious little dance as she tries not to smile.

"Such a prick."

I snatch her hand and bring it to my lips. "Your prick, love."

And I am. I'm hers with every fiber of my being, every molecule of my earthly flesh, and every fleck of stardust in my immortal soul.

I trail kisses up her wrist, reveling in the pulse that flutters and speeds beneath my mouth.

"I have to get to my seminar, James."

"Fuck the seminar," I murmur, snaking a hand around her hip. She slaps my fingers away before I reach her ass.

I'm not giving up yet.

"You could skip every remaining class and they'd still fall over themselves to give you a PhD. You're an internationally bestselling author with several prestigious awards under your belt. Stay home."

Rufus whines in agreement from his cozy spot before the crackling fireplace. *Atta boy!*

"I feel fat today."

I'm so used to the abrupt mental shifts by now that it

only takes a few seconds for me to change gears. Abandoning my physical need for her and ignoring the angry customer in my pants, I kiss her hand a final time.

Meeting her eyes, I take the gift of her vulnerability and give her the only thing I can right now. Words.

"Little muse, you're a beautiful fucking butterfly, remember?"

She groans. "I'm not a butterfly, I'm a flying rodent. And I'm not little—I'm a house!"

I can almost *feel* the quicksand rising around my ankles. But I'm armed for battle. I've got this. I've got *her*.

"Iris Mae Elliot, you are the most ravishing woman in the world. And you're growing the greatest writer in generations in your luscious belly."

She gives me a tentative smile and rubs her palms over her huge stomach. And I won't lie—it's bloody massive. I've managed to keep to myself how proud I am of that fact. I'll let her read it a year from now, when her head's back on straight.

On second thought, maybe I'll hide that particular journal for a decade or three.

Not privy to my thoughts, my lovely wife beams happily at me. "What about the other one?"

I was wondering if she'd catch my omission. *Of*

course she did. She's Iris Eliot. The most brilliant woman in the world, pregnancy-brain notwithstanding.

"Hmm, number two is a bit more of a wildcard. They'll be an artist or dancer, or maybe an astro-physicist."

She sighs in bliss. "Thank you. I feel better now."

Since her belly is taking up most of my vision, I give each of the twins a kiss.

Iris giggles. "You just kissed their feet and butt respectively."

I look up at the love of my life. "If they're anything like you, I'm sure it won't be the last time."

THE END

Stay Connected

www.lmhalloran.com
lm@lmhalloran.com

Acknowledgments

Thank you foremost to the brave men and women who have touched my life with their courage, their perseverance, and their honesty. For L, who taught me that you can find laughter even in the midst of struggle.

To my beta readers, I'd be lost without you! Steph, this one is for you. For Donnie, who's banking on me for early retirement. For Stella, who doesn't yet know what mommy does on the computer and won't know for a while yet (at least another sixteen years), but who I hope will one day be proud to say her mother is a writer.

For my father, who passed away in March of 2017. Thanks to him, my childhood was never short on books. And thank you, always, to my mother, who blushes when she reads my novels but tells all her friends to buy them anyway.

To you, the reader—the life of an indie author isn't glamorous. We need you. *I need you.* So thank you, thank you, thank you, for taking a risk and giving me a chance. I wrote a book I wanted to read, and I hope you enjoyed reading it as much as I enjoyed writing it!

And finally, if you or someone you love has been a victim of sexual assault, please, please pick up the phone. You don't have to feel brave to be brave.

National Sexual Assault Hotline
1-800-656-4673

RAINN
www.rainn.org

Sin of Love (*Illusions Duet #2*)

BILLIONAIRE ROMANCE

The Reluctant Socialite

The Reluctant Heiress

...

URBAN FANTASY / PNR
as LAURA HALL

THE WHITE ORDER

Wellspring

Scroll of Secrets

THE ASCENSION SERIES

Ascension

Reckoning

Unraveling

Rebirth

Tribulation

Revelation

About the Author

When not writing or reading, the author can be found chasing her daughter. Some of her favorite things are puzzles, podcasts, and small dogs that resemble Ewoks.

Home is the Pacific Northwest.

lmhalloran.com

facebook.com/lmhalloran

instagram.com/lm.halloran

tiktok.com/@lmhalloran

pinterest.com/lmhalloranauthor

bookbub.com/authors/l-m-halloran

amazon.com/author/lmhalloran